# BACK WITH A VENGEANCE

# BACK WITH A VENGEANCE

*by*

Glenn Lockwood

**Dales Large Print Books**
Long Preston, North Yorkshire,
BD23 4ND, England.

British Library Cataloguing in Publication Data.

Lockwood, Glenn
    Back with a vengeance.

    A catalogue record of this book is
    available from the British Library

    ISBN   1-84262-148-3 pbk

First published in Great Britain in 2001 by Robert Hale Ltd.

Published in Large Print 2002 by arrangement with
Robert Hale Ltd.

Dales Large Print is an imprint of Library Magna Books Ltd.

Printed and bound in Great Britain by
T.J. (International) Ltd., Cornwall, PL28 8RW

For Janet
Again and Always

# ONE

A man-killer named Charlie Breen rode in first.

He came in from the east astride a frisky buckskin mare, drew rein about midway along Main Street, then swung down and tied up at a nearby rack.

Short and muscular, with dusty blond hair and a square, boyish face – he was, after all, barely more than twenty years old – he stretched briefly to ease the cramps out of his back. Then, adjusting the set of his low-slung Colt Peacemaker, he ambled oh-so-casually across to the little alleyway between the marshal's office and the Colfax Drug-store, where he dug out a machine-made Cross Cut cigarette, lit up and drew smoke deep into his lungs.

As he tipped ash off the end of the cigarette, he studied the thoroughfare carefully from beneath the broad brim of a battered grey hat.

Main Street, Colfax, State of Colorado. A wide, rutted stretch of hardpan that me-

9

andered between facing rows of false-fronted, plank-built stores, saloons, eateries and hotels, with a regular flow of wagon and horseback traffic raising noise and dust to the cloudless morning sky, and a steady procession of townspeople hurrying about their business along each boardwalk.

Spitting a stray flake of tobacco off his lips, he decided that Bowman had called it right yet again. Mining town, he'd said. Tin and copper, mostly, but a bunch of other metals too, whose names Breen couldn't pronounce but which, apparently, had considerable value.

In other words, a *money* town.

And a bank that was packed tight with the stuff.

*But not,* he reminded himself coolly, *for much longer.*

About fifteen minutes later, Ace Hotchkiss – a tall, underfed man with dark, rubbery features, shaggy black hair and loose, sloping shoulders – rode in from the west and dismounted outside the dry goods store next to the bank. As his horse dipped its muzzle to the nearby public trough, Hotchkiss himself studied the bank covertly through hungry, steel-blue eyes.

Big, square and sturdy-looking, constructed from heavy grey-stone slabs eighteen inches thick, with small, high windows screened by fat iron bars and two massive oak doors, it dominated Main Street. But Hotchkiss, thumb-scratching his whiskery jaw thoughtfully, remained unimpressed. An old hand at the stick-up business, he'd seen and robbed too many other banks just like it to think that this one would be any different.

Deciding that the horse had drunk its fill, he tugged the animal a little further along the street, flipped his reins around a tie rack there and went up onto the boardwalk, where he made a big show of admiring the goods displayed in the store window.

Not that he really saw any of them, of course. He was too busy thinking about the money they were just about to take, and all the high times it would buy when the job was done.

The rest of the gang, three men, drifted in ten minutes later.

On the far right came Ed Craven, a big-bellied man of average height who viewed the world from out of one squinty brown eye and a frayed black patch. At forty-six,

11

Craven was the oldest member of the gang. Complex and fidgety, he was also the least predictable. The lower half of his jowly face was covered by a fuzzy, once-red beard that was now shot through with grey, and stained brown around the lips by chewing tobacco. He constantly scratched and tugged at the brittle growth, especially when he was keyed-up, like now.

Slouching in a well-worn Visalia saddle to Craven's far left rode Ned Treber, a tall, broad-faced black man whose wide shoulders strained at the seams of his butternut shirt and calico jacket.

Younger than Craven by a decade, clean-shaven, with flat, dark eyes and a stern, unsmiling mouth, Treber wore his wash-faded Levi's tucked into scuffed, cavalry-issue boots. The hat that covered his kinky glistening hair was cavalry, too: a dark-blue officer's campaign hat. But Treber had never been an officer. Weren't no black officers in the Tenth.

No: the hat was more of a keepsake, a memento of the white officer who'd caught him in the act of deserting five years earlier, and whom Treber had run through with his own three-foot, two-inch sabre during the scuffle that followed.

He'd kept the sabre, too, and still carried it with him in a shiny silver scabbard affixed to the left side of his gunbelt.

The fifth and final member of the gang sat his big sabino horse between the two men, and of them all, he was perhaps the most dangerous. Tall and powerfully built, with a narrow, weathered face cut in two by a massive black longhorn moustache, Arch Bowman was the son of a Baptist minister who'd left home young and quickly drifted into bad company. Intelligent, selfish and apparently unburdened by conscience, he had been taught to kill and to enjoy killing during the late war, and had since honed his skills as a widow-maker with the single-action Frontier model Colt .44 he carried in the functional R. E. Rice holster on his right thigh. Bowman was wanted in four states and as many territories, for everything from bastardy to murder.

Together, Bowman, Treber and Craven continued to walk their horses slowly along Main, their eyes – or, in the case of Craven, *eye* – constantly scanning the boardwalks to either side for any sign of trouble. But, as Charlie Breen had already noted, Colfax was a busy town. Nameless men of all types came and went twenty-four hours a day, so

13

no one paid much attention to the trail-dusted, weapon-heavy newcomers.

Bowman slowly raised his very dark, close-set eyes to the bank. It was baking in the pleasant mid-morning heat, its narrow shadow tucked in nice and neat at the base of the facing wall. Then he threw a casual glance toward the Colfax Drugstore and, when he saw Charlie Breen take the cigarette butt out of his mouth and toss it away, the broad, almost lipless mouth beneath his moustache worked in a brief tic, because that gesture meant, *No law in sight.*

They pushed on, angled their horses up to the tie rack outside the bank, dismounted and tied up loosely. As Ed Craven reached into his near-side saddle-bag and drew out two empty flour sacks, Bowman caught a glance from Ned Treber. For just a moment their eyes met, and Bowman saw the light of excitement in those of his companion.

Briefly then, he wondered why he himself no longer shared that same sense of anticipation. He couldn't even remember when the excitement had stopped and the emptiness had started. Now he just felt ... nothing. None of the nervous fear that had been coursing through Craven since sunrise, none of the perverse pleasure Treber took in robbing white folks, none of Charlie Breen's youthful excitement, or the short-sighted, obsessive greed of Ace Hotchkiss. For Bowman, robbery was no longer a novelty. It was just a chore – and an irksome one, at that.

In the next moment, however, he shoved the problem aside. It was, after all, of little consequence. And in this game, concentration on the job at hand was everything.

He stepped up onto the boardwalk and started for the doorway, Treber and Craven following right behind him. As they went, each man's free hand moved automatically to the bandanna hanging around his neck. By the time they'd let themselves inside the bank, they were all masked from the nose down.

On the other side of the tall double doors they found a big room with a high ceiling, dark-panelled walls and knotty oak floor-boards that smelled of wax polish. Sunshine slanted in through the barred, green-shaded windows to illuminate two tables upon which inkwells, pens and withdrawal and deposit slips had been set out for the convenience of the bank's customers. Just beyond the tables, a handful of those same customers – men, mostly, but a couple of women, as well – were lined up in front of a small, three-sided box counter that was perhaps nine feet square and butted up nice and snug to the back wall. Two neatly attired clerks in grey suits and celluloid collars were carrying out the day's transactions behind a flimsy grille that was constructed from thin, impractical slats of gold-painted wood, and behind them stood a half-open door upon which was painted, in fancy script, the legend, GEORGE HOBART, MGR.

Bowman and Craven drew and cocked their revolvers, then walked quickly across the room. Ned Treber stayed just inside the doorway, where he could keep an eye on the street.

'Aw right, folks!' snapped Bowman, his hard, gravelly voice suddenly filling the near silence. 'Get y'hands up, now, an' get over agin yonder wall!'

Heads turned quickly, almost in unison, and Bowman found himself confronted with all the usual expressions: surprise, confusion, fear. He said again, irritably, 'Get up agin yonder wall!' And to make them do as he said, he stepped in fast and pistol-whipped the nearest man in line with a single, savage swipe.

That got them moving and, as they

16

shuffled over to the far wall, one of them helping to support the bloody-mouthed man Bowman had just struck, Craven took over, handing the flour sacks to Bowman and then jabbing his Remington .44-.40 at the pale-faced customers with a gun-hand that trembled faintly. 'D-d-don't you gimme no tr-trouble, now!' he stammered. 'I ain't a'f-feared to use this!'

Bowman crossed to the box counter, his bootfalls loud and hollow against the waxed boards, his long grey duster swishing around his calves. When he got there, he thrust his .44 at the two startled clerks, threw the sacks onto the counter and said in a voice faintly muffled by the bandanna, 'You know the routine. All you got – right now.'

One of the clerks, a youngish fellow with slicked-back hair and a pencil neck, bobbed his head. He seemed unable to tear his gaze away from the revolver in Bowman's fist. Nervously, he opened one of the sacks and told his companion to start filling it with bills of all denominations.

Bowman watched them work, noting the way they fumbled time and again in their hurry to please him. Once, he'd have enjoyed the fear he and his .44 inspired so easily in others. Once, a bank job like this would've made him feel like the biggest man in the territory. Now, though...

The big, yellow-faced wall-clock above the door slowly ticked away the seconds. Tock-tock ... tock-tock... The man Bowman had pistol whipped spat out teeth and sobbed softly. Another frightened customer coughed, and Craven, shoulders hunched, gun-hand still shaking, said, 'I'm w-watchin' you, mister! No tr-tricks, now! You j-jus' sh-show me a little respect here, you g-got that?' And with his free hand he reached under his bandanna and started tugging nervously at his fuzzy beard.

The clerk with the pencil neck passed the first flour sack back to Bowman. It fairly bulged with money. He took it, felt the weight of it and wanted it to do something for him, to stir something within him, the way it used to. But it did nothing, and the nothingness made him feel a little sick.

'The street?' he called over one shoulder.

'Ever'thin's jus' fine heah,' replied Treber, without turning his head.

Bowman thought, *Good*, then hurried the two clerks along with a raspy, 'Come on, come on...'

Just then, the door behind the clerks swung all the way open and a short, portly man in a black suit and a neatly-tied blue cravat came hurrying into the poky box counter. Bowman tensed immediately and his fingers whitened around the .44, but seeing only a prissy-looking fifty-year-old with bloodshot eyes and thinning grey hair – almost certainly George Hobart, the manager – he allowed himself to relax again.

That was a big mistake.

Hobart came to a halt between the clerks and demanded, 'What is the meaning of this?'

And then he brought up the short-barrelled Cooper pocket pistol he'd been holding close to his right leg and yelled, *'Down, everyone!'*

The double-action handgun thundered in his pink fist and a .31-calibre slug drilled right through the splayed hand Bowman had been using to hold the money-filled flour sack against his chest. It bored on through the flour sack itself and finally came to rest in the fatty flesh just below his ribs.

One of the women over by the far wall screamed and, twisting around, Ed Craven said, dumbly, 'W-what–'

The bullet rocked Bowman back a pace, but didn't knock him all the way over. For a long, sluggish moment he just stood there, his shock-widened eyes fixed on the bank manager, who began to look a little scared. He dropped the flour sack, grabbed at his left hip and felt warm blood begin to puddle in a ruined palm that was already overflowing with the stuff.

Then–

'You little bastard,' he breathed, and aiming the .44 at Hobart, pulled the trigger.

His bullet slammed through the flimsy wooden grille and punched an inch-wide hole in the bank manager's chest. As he shot Hobart a second time, blood leapt from the wound like a crimson snake to splash wetly on the floorboards at the man's feet, and there followed another scream as Hobart collapsed in a quivering heap.

All at once, the bank was in uproar. Both women were screaming now, and all the men were yelling. Craven, shifting his weight from one foot to the other, shouted, *'Sh-shut up! Sh-shut up, damn you!'* But no one took any notice.

Ned Treber pushed away from the door, crossed the room at a run that made his sabre bang noisily against his left leg, and caught Bowman just as he started to collapse. 'Jesus!' he whispered. Then, 'Ed, grab the sack!'

Knowing they had to get out of there fast, he started dragging Bowman across to the doorway. Behind him, he heard Craven shouting, 'N-no-one move, now! N-no-one move!'

Bowman's feet slipped on the waxed floorboards. His face was absolutely bloodless, his close-set eyes big and glazed. Struggling with him, Treber kept muttering, 'C'mon, man, you kin do it. *Tha's* the way...' Inside the box counter, the two clerks looked uncertainly from their dead boss to the escaping robbers.

Craven came up on the far side of Bowman just as they reached the doorway, the money-filled, blood-spattered flour sack clutched in his free hand. Bowman chose that precise moment to lose consciousness altogether, and suddenly Treber was struggling to support his full weight.

'H-h-he's dead!' squealed Craven.

'The hell he's dead!'

'He's *d-dead*, I tell you!' stuttered Craven, the single, squinty eye visible above his bandanna shuttling this way and that like a loosely-packed brown marble. 'L-l-leave him! H-he'll only s-slow us down!'

Treber said murderously, 'Jus' get that goddam door open, an' shoot anyone tries to stop us!'

Dipping his head, Craven did as he was told.

The three gunshots had pretty much cleared the immediate vicinity, but a big, heavily put-together man in a tall, broad-brimmed hat was just hurrying out of the marshal's office and jumping down off the boardwalk with a rifle in his fists as they stumbled outside.

Even as they hauled up sharp, another gunblast echoed along Main and the lawman staggered, folded sideways in on himself and fell to his knees in the dirt, the rifle dropping from his grasp as a crimson rose blossomed just below his brassy law-dog's badge. A second man, younger and smaller than the first, followed him outside, twisted and dropped to one knee in the middle of the plankwalk. He slammed the stock of a .44-.40 to his cheek and threw a quick shot back at Charlie Breen, who'd just downed his boss.

Standing his ground, too damn' young or too damn' crazy to be scared, Breen only giggled and fanned his Peacemaker back at the deputy. Boardwalk wood splintered all around the man, and stone chips spanged off the nearby law-office wall to rake at his

22

face. Instinctively, the deputy thrust himself back to his feet, intending to grab cover – and that was when Ace Hotchkiss got him.

The minute all hell started breaking loose, the lean, rubber-featured man had leapt for his horse and dragged his chunky Winchester shotgun from the saddle-scabbard. Now he worked the lever, snap-aimed and hit the deputy from the side and a little behind. The blast of the shot roared through Colfax, and the shot itself pretty much shredded the deputy and slammed him hard against the law-office wall. He hung there for a moment, bleeding from at least half-a-dozen separate wounds, then slid down to the boardwalk and didn't move again.

Down in the street itself, the marshal finally collapsed on his face.

Outside the bank, Treber and Craven started dragging Bowman's limp body across to the stamping horses. The tips of Bowman's boots made a deep, rolling sound as they scraped across the warped boards. Still clutching the bloodstained flour sack, Craven helped to carry the unconscious man as far as the tie rack, then ducked out from under Bowman's right arm, threw himself into the saddle and yelled, 'C-come! C-come on!'

'Gimme a hand heah!' bawled Treber.

But then Ace Hotchkiss was beside him, his shotgun fisted in one hand. Between them, they boosted Bowman across his saddle, where his hat fell off and rolled away. Treber thought, hell with that. Then he himself was mounting up and grabbing Bowman's reins in his free hand; Hotchkiss was running back to his own horse, and across the street, Charlie Breen was swinging astride his feisty buckskin mare.

Perhaps a little more civic-minded than his fellow townsmen, a black-haired man in shirt-sleeves and a brocade vest came out onto the plankwalk in front of the Lucky Dollar Saloon, levelled a Henry repeater at the outlaws and pulled the trigger. Drawing a long-barrelled Colt .45, Ned Treber hurled a shot back at him and yelled, *'Ride!'*

Unbowed, the man outside the Lucky Dollar Saloon fired the Henry again. Later Craven would swear he felt the wind of the bullet as it whined past his head and smacked into a porch-post behind him.

Whipping at his horse with his split-ended reins, he yelled, *'Yaaahhh!'* And together, he and his companions galloped out of Colfax with bullets chasing their heels.

24

They rode north, across a great, rising belt of deep green grassland and on into thickly forested high country. As near as Treber could tell, there was no pursuit, but he kept them moving anyway, because they'd left three dead men behind them, and past experience had taught him that townsfolk took things like that to heart.

The day wore on. The timber fell behind them and a vast, lichen-encrusted boulder field stretched ahead. In the distance, a series of irregular-shaped buttes shelved skyward, showing dull grey and flat brown in the coming, pink-and-purple sunset.

Early evening found them camped in a scrubby clearing surrounded by Engelmann spruce. Here, Breen and Hotchkiss slid Bowman down off his blood-soaked saddle and stretched him out, none too gently, on a bed of bluegrass mottled with russet-coloured strawberry leaves. 'Ace,' called Treber, kneeling beside the unconscious man and peeling back his bloodstained duster, 'get a fire goin' so I kin see what I'm lookin' at heah.'

A few minutes later, Treber was studying the extent of Bowman's injuries by the flickering light of a flaming torch. Behind him, Charlie Breen lit and smoked a Cross

Cut cigarette and Ed Craven scratched anxiously at his whiskers, the pair of them watching the examination with much curiosity, but little noticeable compassion.

George Hobart's small-calibre slug had punched a neat hole barely more than half an inch wide through the centre of Bowman's left hand. Now, the puffy wound was blue and faintly puckered around the edges. There wasn't much that Treber felt he could do for it, just clean it up, bandage it and hope it didn't turn bad. The hole just below Bowman's ribcage, by contrast, was altogether more serious, because Bowman had lost a lot of blood from it, and the bullet had to come out before they could plug it and keep him from losing any more.

Craven asked, 'Is he g-gonna die?'

By way of reply, Treber said, 'Charlie, go fetch my kit.'

'F-five bucks says he d-dies,' muttered Craven, but no one took him up on the wager.

Treber's kit turned out to be a long strip of soft, tied buckskin in which were wrapped a few surgical irons he'd stolen one time, and a bottle of 120° proof Everclear Grain. Treber washed his hands in a little of the liquor, then used a drop more to clean

Bowman's hand, which he then wrapped in a length of torn shirt donated, albeit reluctantly, by Craven. When he started cleaning the chest wound, the sting of it brought Bowman back to a hazy kind of consciousness.

'...Whu ... what–'

''S'awright, Arch. You aw right now.'

'I been shot?'

'Yeah, but I'm goan fix that.'

Bowman nodded, swallowed a slug of Everclear and choked on the fiery mixture of pure alcohol, burnt sugar and crushed peaches. When his mind cleared again, he thought emptily, yeah, Ned's gonna fix it. Ned was gonna patch him up so that he could carry on living this dead kind of life from which all purpose had vanished.

Hardly seemed worth the effort, somehow.

He took another long pull at the Everclear, and another, and one more. Then he heard Treber say, 'This is gonna hurt some.'

'Course it was gonna hurt. Wasn't much in life – *his* life, anyway – that *didn't* hurt.

He took another pull at the bottle before an unseen hand took it away from him. Then he felt the boys grabbing his arms and shoulders, holding him steady, and someone else sitting across his legs. He waited, bracing himself and, after a moment, Treber selected a long, thin and not entirely clean probe from the kit and went in search of the bullet.

As the probe slid inexpertly into the wound, Bowman screamed loud enough to wake the dead.

They spent the next two days just after waiting to see whether or not Bowman would live or die, and when he didn't oblige them by living or dying right away, Ed Craven started scratching fretfully at his beard.

'I d-don't like this h-hangin' around,' he complained. 'I s-say we should k-keep on the move.'

No one paid him any mind. No one *ever* paid him any mind. Once, he'd been a dirt farmer, a spectacularly unsuccessful one. And sometimes it seemed that failure had been the story of his entire life. Everyone he'd ever known had treated him like a nobody, until that one particular day when he'd told himself, no more. Respect, that's what he craved more than anything else. And the best thing about riding the owlhoot was that, when you held a gun in your hand, folks gave you all the respect you could ever want.

There was, however, a problem: he'd

always been jumpy; it was in his nature, and the uncertain, violent life of the outlaw terrified him. But he was too hungry for respect to give it up.

In his rumpled blankets, meanwhile, Bowman continued to sweat and shiver. Beneath his moustache, his teeth clamped hard, and his fever-induced nightmares brought a constant frown to his brow, and the occasional, troubled moan to his lips.

*'Damn you, woman! What more can I do?'*

*'You can settle down, Arch! You can give up all your wild ways and–'*

*'The hell I'll let you tell me how to live my life!'*

*A laugh. A harsh, derisive, sad little laugh. 'You still don't understand, you, Arch?'*

*'What's there to understand?'*

*'That it's not just about what you want any more...'*

Another day and a half passed, and then the fever broke and left him. He opened bloodshot eyes, saw a clear night sky sprinkled with faint, glittering stars. He lay there awhile, just thinking about what had happened to him, remembering who he was, puzzling everything out slowly and laboriously. Then, turning his head a little, he saw a low, rock-ringed camp-fire, and four familiar silhouettes drinking coffee.

He tried to speak, but all that came out was a parched kind of gurgle. It got their attention, though, and suddenly they were gathered around him, and Treber was holding a canteen to his cracked lips.

He drank greedily, until Treber took the canteen away and said, 'Easy, now, easy...'

Bowman choked a little and lay back, breathing hard.

'How you feelin' now?' asked Treber.

He cleared his throat, considered the question and rasped, ''Bout as ... weak as Ed's coffee.'

'That's no surprise. You lost a lot o' blood.'

'You got the ... bullet, though?'

Treber nodded. 'You was lucky.'

'I don't ... feel so lucky.'

Treber said soberly, 'Iffen that slug hadn't gone through yo' left hand first, an' then on through that sack o' money you was holdin', it would'a kilt you outright.'

Bowman frowned. Hand? He raised his left arm slowly, inspected it curiously. The hand was wrapped in a strip of soiled, blood-smeared shirt. He tried to move his fingers, but couldn't.

'You rest up awhile,' said Treber. 'You goan be aw right now, Arch.'

They went back to the fire, leaving him to frown up at the distant stars and think again about what Treber had just told him. But for a freak accident, he'd have been dead by now, killed by a prissy looking little bank manager with a lousy pocket pistol in his fist.

But he *wasn't* dead. He was still here.

Why?

His dark, close-set eyes continued to move thoughtfully from one star to another as he tried to puzzle it out. He remembered the way the wall-clock in the bank had ticked away the seconds of each man's life. Tock-tock … tock-tock… And he remembered something else he'd only half-heard: *F-five bucks says he d-dies.*

Was that all his life was worth? Five bucks?

He wasn't afraid to die. But to die unmourned and unloved, as he would, to be forgotten almost as soon as his coffin was six feet under, to die without leaving anything of worth behind to prove that he'd ever lived…

Suddenly it came to him why he'd been spared. This past year or two, his life had been entirely without purpose. But not any more. For all at once, Arch Bowman had become a man with a mission.

A terrible, *terrible* mission.

# TWO

Walt Canaday woke earlier than usual that morning, shoved off his blanket, swung his long legs over the side of the barley-straw mattress and then sat for a while with his head buried in his hands.

Today, he thought a little sickly, was the day. And, for what seemed like the millionth time, he asked himself if he was sure he was doing the right thing. After all, it was a big step to take. There was so much that could go wrong, and—

And nothing, he told himself more firmly, and deliberately squared his shoulders to at least give the impression of confidence. It was too late to turn back now, even if he'd been of a mind, which he wasn't. So...

He stood up, a tall man whose lean, work toughened body was encased in faded red longjohns, and went across to the window, where he peered out into the chilly pre-dawn. Beyond the smeared glass, and far beyond the neat fields of winter wheat, maize and sugar beet that were his liveli-

33

hood, the hill country of south-western Nebraska stood in silhouette against the grey horizon.

Lord, he thought wretchedly, I'm not sure I can go through with this. But that was just nerves talking. If you looked at it logically, there was no good reason why this thing shouldn't pan out just dandy. After all, folks could hardly say that he'd rushed into it. He'd thought it through just as slowly and carefully as he thought through 'most everything.

But still the doubts persisted, as did the unpleasant churning of his stomach.

He went back to the bed, lifted his best pair of snug-fitting black trousers off the footboard and stepped into them. Next, he stamped into and laced up his ankle jacks. Then, still shivering a little, he went through the sleeping house to the covered porch out back, visited the necessary, pumped out a bowl of icy water and began to lather his face at a small, condensation-beaded mirror nailed to one of the porch-posts.

The face that stared back at him looked somewhat older than its thirty-six years, but then, this land had a way of using people up long before their time. His hazel eyes were honest and well spaced, his nose long and straight, his mouth generous, if a little sad. The chin was strong and firm, the ears small, the longish hair a sun-bleached, wheaty colour. He frowned when he thought of that word, *longish*, and made a mental note to get it cut when he reached town.

Tilting his head a little, he shaved slowly, with more care than usual, then reached for his towel and patted himself dry. Finished at last, he threw the damp towel across one broad shoulder, turned to go back inside – and found Matt watching him silently from the back doorway.

Already jumpy, he started a little, then said gently, ''Mornin' son.'

Matt nodded cautiously. ''Mornin, Pa.'

'You're up early.'

'You, too.'

'Big day today, I guess. Couldn't sleep much for thinkin' of it.'

'Me, neither.'

Something in the boy's attitude, something in his voice, made Walt frown. He stepped up onto the porch, put a calloused hand on Matt's shoulder and said quietly, 'You're not *worried* about this, are you, son?'

Matt shook his head, suddenly looking much younger than his fifteen years. He was tall and lean, just like his father, but there the similarity ended. Matt, like his sister Joey, had his mother's dark-brown hair, the exact same shade, and her same shrewd green eyes. In fact, brother and sister reminded Walt so much of Kate that sometimes it almost hurt him just to look at them.

'I know things're bound to change around here,' he continued awkwardly, 'but...'

Matt looked up at him, his green eyes giving nothing away.

Looking back at him, Walt cursed his inadequacy. There was so much he wanted to say, but he just didn't know how to say it. So, all he said was, 'Just remember this, Matt: no matter what happens, I'll always be your father, and you'll always be my son. Nothing'll ever change that.'

'You promise?' asked Matt, adding hastily, 'It's, ah, not for me that I'm askin'. It's Joey an' Sam. They think ... they're worried you won't...' He shook his head, frustrated that he couldn't articulate his own concerns.

Walt saved him the trouble. 'You just remember what I said,' he replied gently. 'An' you tell Joey an' Sam, too, so there won't be no doubts about it. You're my younkers, the three of you. You'll *always* be my younkers, even when you're all old an' grey an' got younkers of your own.'

Matt laughed a little self-consciously. 'They'll be glad to hear that, Pa.'

Walt squeezed his son's shoulder. 'An' you?'

The boy's response was a casual shrug. 'Aw, I wasn't worried.'

Walt smiled down at him. ''Course you weren't.' Then he put one arm around the boy's shoulders and led him back inside. 'Come on,' he said with new purpose. 'The day's gettin' started, an' I got a stagecoach to meet.'

He slipped into a collarless white shirt, buttoned up, tucked in and then shrugged his wide blue suspenders up over his shoulders. By the time he came back into the combination parlour and kitchen, with its rug-covered puncheon floor and huge rock fireplace, Joey and Sam were up and about, and the good breakfast smells of buckwheat pancakes, hung beef, hot bread and eggs was rich in the air.

When they all sat down at the black walnut table, however, there was only one topic of conversation, and it had nothing to do with food. 'How long you gonna be away, Pa?' asked Joey, who was twelve.

'Just for tonight,' he said. 'Be back early tomorrow.'

Joey studied him from beneath lowered brows, her expression, almost comically serious as she asked, 'You sure?'

He reached over and scrubbed at her long auburn hair. 'You know somethin', Miss Josephine?' he replied. 'This seems to be my day for makin' promises. But I guess one more won't hurt.'

Later he hitched the two-horse team to the small box wagon, put on a rusty black jacket – the same one he'd worn to Kate's funeral – and finally said his goodbyes. 'Now, you all got your chores to do. Sam, you fed them hens yet?'

Sam was nine years old, a sturdy boy with a fiery mop of hair and a butterfly-shaped spill of freckles across his snub nose. 'Yes, Pa.'

'Don't forget the hogs – or your studies. And remember what I told you, Matt: any problems, you ride on over to Jack Partlett's place, you hear me?'

'I hear you, Pa.'

He settled his loose-brimmed black hat firmly atop his head, then bent so that he could scoop Joey into his arms and nuzzle the side of her face, which always made her

38

giggle. Then he turned to Sam, who stood before him with his right hand extended stiffly.

'So long, Pa,' said the boy, formally.

With much solemnity, Walt went down on one knee, took the hand and shook with him. Then, without warning, he yanked Sam towards him and gave him a hug, too. 'You kids take care, now,' he said when he finally let the boy go. 'I'll be back just as soon as I can.'

As he climbed onto the high seat and gathered up the lines, Matt called softly, 'Pa?'

'Son?'

The boy said, almost confidentially, 'We won't let you down tomorrow. We'll be on our best behaviour.' Then he grinned a little and added, 'That's my promise to *you*.'

''Preciate it, son. It means a lot to me.'

He hesitated for just a moment longer, to survey the farm. The single-storey house, the shed and barn, the hen-house and hog-pen, were all in a good state of repair. He'd built them all with his own two hands, had erected each thin timber frame in such a way as to conserve wood, and then nailed every tarred plank carefully into place. He'd fixed every red shingle to every pitched roof and saved every spare cent just so's he could give his family the luxury of real glass windows as soon as possible. He'd cultivated a fine vegetable patch and dug down forty back-breaking feet to find water that he could then pipe through to the kitchen and out back. And now, looking at all he'd achieved, and taking pride in his accomplishments, he suddenly felt more confident than he had a couple of hours earlier.

The journey to town – its name was Freedom Rock, though he had no idea why – took him up through the empty hills and on across rolling grass plains that were featureless save for the odd stand of elm or cottonwood. As the morning wore on, a hot wind sprang up from the south-west and sent the temperature soaring. He felt sweaty inside his jacket, but kept it on because he thought it smartened him up some, and he'd read once about just how important first impressions could be.

He reached Freedom Rock shortly after noon. The town was little more than a wide strip of wheel-rutted hardpan across which one row of false-fronted, plank-built stores, saloons and boarding-houses could face and compete with another. At the far north-eastern tip of town, just across from the church, he parked the wagon along the side wall of Bill Summerfield's livery stable and paid in advance for the overnight care of his team-animals.

'Not often we see you in town,' remarked Summerfield, who was a garrulous, good-natured little man with scraggy black hair and crooked teeth. 'Come to think of it, not often we get to see you all gussied-up, neither. What's the occasion, Walt?'

'Meetin' my intended,' Walt muttered self-consciously.

Summerfield paused in the act of unhitching the team and said wonderingly, 'You don't say! Finally gettin' to meet that gal you been writin' to all these months, huh? Well, I wish you all the luck Walt, I really do. I always did say a man without a woman was a sad thing, 'specially when he's got three kids to raise—' He broke off abruptly and eyed Walt sidelong as a new thought occurred to him. 'This the first time you've met this here lady?'

'Uh-huh.'

'So you don't even know what she looks like?'

'Nope. She never did get to have her picture made.'

Summerfield went back to unhitching the

41

team, remarking with a chuckle, 'Well, it's a brave man takes on a blind proposition like that. She got a name, the future Mrs Canaday?'

'Ellie – uh, that is, Eleanor. Eleanor Bryant.'

'Widder-woman or spinster, Walt?'

'Neither one. Just a woman lookin' to start a new life.'

'Comin' far to start it, is she?'

'All the way from Minnesota. Place called St Cloud.'

'Well, when she gets here, you make sure you fetch her by to say hello, you hear me? We'll make her as welcome as we can, I reckon.'

As Walt stepped back onto the street, he felt some of his earlier anxiety returning. Bill was right. A blind proposition, he'd called it. And that was exactly what Walt was letting himself in for. He'd corresponded with Ellie – she'd told him early on that she preferred that name to the more formal Eleanor – for eight months, and knew about her only what she'd chosen to tell him. He himself had been completely honest – it was the only way he knew *how* to be – and he'd naturally assumed that she would be, too. But what if she'd spun him a pack of lies instead? What was he *really* letting himself – and, more importantly, his children – in for?

All at once he wanted to turn around, tell Bill to hitch up the wagon and get the hell out of town as fast as he could. But he knew that Bill had been right about something else, too: a man without a woman *was* a sad thing. And there were his younkers to think about, growing up out there on the farm, without a mother's love to make the isolation any easier for them to bear.

In any case, he reminded himself testily, it was a little late to start having second thoughts now, wasn't it? Sure it was. Which meant that, for better or worse, he was stuck with Miss Ellie Bryant from St Cloud, Minnesota.

Or was he?

His troubled hazel eyes suddenly came to rest on the combination Western Union and US Post Office on the other side of the street. Suppose Ellie'd had second thoughts herself? Or just plain chickened out? It was possible. If she *had*, it could be that he'd find a letter waiting for him over there right now, apologizing and cancelling all the arrangements they'd made.

As he crossed hurriedly to the flimsy little

43

clapboard building, he kind of hoped he was right.

The office was operated by a balding, bearded clerk-telegraphist named Bernie Wilkes. Bernie was sorting mail into a row of pigeonholes when Walt let himself inside and, when he heard the door open, then close, he glanced over one shoulder to identify the newcomer. 'Uh, 'afternoon, Mr Canaday. How can I help you?'

Swallowing hard, Walt said casually, 'Any, ah, mail for me today?' And he thought, yes. Please say yes. And please let it be what I want it to be.

But Bernie said, 'Nary a thing, Mr Canaday. An' before you enquire, no telegrams, neither. I fear the line must've come down again late las' night or early this mornin'.'

Barely able to hide his disappointment, Walt replied vaguely. 'Sorry to hear that. I, ah … I guess that makes life difficult for you, huh?'

'Like you wouldn't *believe*.'

Nodding his thanks, Walt let himself back out onto the street, where he walked, unseeing, straight into Pat Patterson.

'Whoa, there!' said the marshal of Freedom Rock, grabbing Walt by the arms to

44

steady them both.

Walt backed off a pace. 'Uh, sorry 'bout that, Pat. Guess I just wasn't–'

'Forget it, no harm done. But... Christ, you all right, Walt?'

'Sure. Why?'

'You look like hell, is why.'

It was then that Pat – his real name was Dave, but nobody ever called him that – noticed the clean white shirt, the best black pants, the ankle jacks and the rusty black jacket, and suddenly understanding dawned in his pleasant blue eyes.

'Don't tell me,' he said, grinning. 'Today's the big day, is it?'

Walt sighed irritably. 'If you mean, today's the day I meet Miss Bryant, yeah.'

Pat leaned back to examine him with head cocked critically. He was a tall, tough, beefy man of an age with Walt, dressed in a wash-faded blue shirt and string tie, creased Levi's tucked into tan-coloured, stovepipe work-boots and a grey hat which he wore with the front brim folded back off his forehead. 'Yep,' he said at last. 'You look about as nervous as a long-tailed cat in a room full o' rockers.'

A sour smile touched Walt's broad mouth. 'Then I look just about how I feel.'

45

'Aw, don't fret none, Walt. It'll all work out fine.'

'Sure it will.'

'I *mean* it,' the marshal said more firmly. He had a long, weathered face, generous, triangular-shaped sideburns and neatly-trimmed mouse-brown hair. 'Listen to me, iffen this here Miz Bryant's half the woman Kate was, you got no worries – she'll make you a fine wife.'

'Sure she will. But what if she *isn't?*'

With a sigh, Pat took an Ingersoll watch from the pocket of his buttoned, leather-trimmed waistcoat, snapped it open and checked the time. 'Come on,' he said. 'I'll buy you a coffee. Stage ain't due for another–'

He stiffened suddenly, his gaze sharpening on something behind Walt and, as the warmth faded from his blue eyes, he seemed to grow somehow taller and more tense.

Frowning at him, Walt murmured, 'What...?'

Then he turned and looked away to the south-west, where five horsemen, riding line abreast, were just entering Main Street at a dusty walk.

He ran his eyes from one man to the next, saw a blocky, square-faced kid with blond

46

hair, a big-bellied man with a patch over one eye who kept scratching furiously at his fuzzy, copper-coloured beard, a wide-shouldered man with a narrow face and a massive longhorn moustache, a long-legged Negro with a cavalry sword bumping gently against his left leg, and a lanky, skinny-built man with dark, shaggy hair showing beneath his sugarloaf sombrero, and a rubbery, stubbled face.

Still frowning, he said, 'Trouble?'

Pat shook his head faintly, snapped the Ingersoll shut and put it away. 'Don't know,' he said at last. 'Could be.'

As the newcomers drew nearer, the man at the centre of the line, whose powerful frame was hidden beneath a voluminous grey duster, raised his left hand to the brim of his hat in greeting. Walt noticed the hand was bandaged crudely. Beside him, Pat threw a cautious nod back at the man.

Then the five horsemen angled in to the tie rack outside Len Parsons' Freedom Saloon, dismounted, tied up and clattered tiredly inside. Only when they were out of sight did some of the stiffness drain out of Pat's shoulders.

'What was we sayin'?' he asked.

'You was just about to buy me a cup o'

47

coffee, but I got some things to do before the stage gets here.'

Pat forced a smile. 'Church's right behind you, iffen prayin's one of 'em.'

Distracted as he was, even Walt had to laugh. 'Way I feel right now,' he allowed, 'even that's worth a try, I reckon.'

Pat put a big, work-roughened palm on his shoulder and gave him a little shake. 'It'll all work out fine,' he said quietly. 'You know it will.'

Walt nodded and calming down again, said, 'You get on about your business; me, I got to get a haircut.'

But by then Pat had put his blue eyes back on the five horses tied up outside the Freedom Saloon, and was rubbing his square jaw thoughtfully.

Bowman and his cronies shoved in through the squeaky batwing doors and took a long, searching look around the saloon. It was a remarkably plain saloon, as saloons went. There were no frills here, just a short, roughly hammered-together oak bar, three shelves that sagged beneath the weight of all kinds of bottled beverages, a clutch of scratched and chipped tables and chairs and a few strategically placed, dented and tarnished spittoons.

Neither was the Freedom doing much in the way of lunchtime trade: the big, plank-built room was empty but for two men down at the far end of the bar, who were nursing shot-glasses and conversing in low tones, and a chunky man in a white shirt and sleeve protectors, who pushed himself upright and gave the bartop a quick, perfunctory polish as the newcomers filled the doorway.

Bowman indicated a table that was tucked away in the far right-hand corner and, while his companions crossed the splintery, sawdusted boards to reach it, he himself strode stiffly toward the bar, still favouring his healing wound.

'Name your disturbance, friend,' invited the bartender, who was also the owner of the place, Len Parsons.

'A bottle of Old Crow an' four glasses,' said Bowman, thumbing some coins onto the counter.

'Come far?' asked Parsons, with professional interest.

'Far enough,' Bowman replied curtly, and taking the liquor across to the corner table, set it down and said to his companions, 'See you directly.'

Ned Treber frowned up at him from beneath the brim of his old Army campaign hat. 'Where you goin', Arch?'

'Take a look around town,' said Bowman. He glanced at Ace Hotchkiss and added, 'Saw a decent-lookin' hotel on the way in, Ace. When you've killed that bottle, go book us a couple rooms.'

Hotchkiss nodded. 'Sure.'

While Charlie Breen opened the bottle and poured four generous shots, Treber watched Bowman head for the batwings and push out into the hot, bright afternoon with nary a backward glance. Beside him, Hotchkiss asked quietly, 'What's the deal, Ned? Whyfore we come to this stinkin' little one-horse town, an' how long we stayin'?'

Treber said flatly, 'Wisht I knew.'

'Me, I reckon it's the bank,' opined Charlie Breen. 'We're gonna take the bank.'

Ed Craven itched at his fuzzy chin. 'Well, w-whatever it is, I d-don't like it,' he stammered. 'You s-see the way that l-lawdog was w-watchin' us on the w-way in, Ned?'

Treber took his glass and made no reply. But he'd meant what he'd said a few moments earlier. He wished he *did* know what was going on inside Arch's head, but, for once, Bowman had chosen not to confide in him.

They'd spent a week holed up in the timbered high country, while Bowman recovered from Treber's crude surgery. He hadn't said much in all that time, just sat and brooded.

The rest of the boys had hated such a prolonged spell of inactivity. With the proceeds of the Colfax bank robbery burning a hole in each man's pocket, they could think of a lot of things they'd sooner be doing than killing every interminable day out in the middle of nowhere. 'Course, they knew better than to come right out and say as much, leastways to Bowman's face. Bowman wouldn't have taken kindly to that, even weak and wounded as he was.

After the first few days, the weather had turned bad – squally winds and heavy rain – and Treber had got them to rig up a crude kind of brush arbour before discontent could turn into outright mutiny. Then, as they huddled around a low, fitful fire one dark, damp, wind-swept night, Bowman finally broke his long silence.

'Any o' you fellers ever think about dyin'?'

It was such a profound and unexpected question that Charlie Breen, still so young that he thought he'd live forever, answered it with a giggle.

'N-no, Arch's right,' said Ed Craven nervously. 'I m-mean, we all got it c-comin'. A m-man *should* think about his own m-mortality ever' once in a while.'

Ace Hotchkiss shook his head. 'Tha' where you' wrong, ol'-timer. A man ought to occupy his thoughts with livin', I reckon. He starts thinkin' 'bout the other, he's apt to wind up too scairt to do *anythin'*.'

'Whyfore you ask such a question, Arch?' asked Treber.

Bowman glanced at him above the rim of his enamel coffee cup. 'You been laid up before,' he said. 'A man gets plenty time to think. Too much time. Anyway, I don't mean dyin', exactly, I mean more ... what happens after you're dead.'

'You m-mean Heaven, an' that?' asked Craven.

'I mean, what does a man leave behind him?'

Hotchkiss shrugged. 'Men like us, you mean?' He thought about it for a moment, then said, 'He leaves his name. His reputation.'

Bowman nodded. 'An' how long do *they* last?'

The next morning he pronounced himself fit enough to ride. The relief of the other men was almost palpable. As they started to break camp, Charlie Breen said, 'Where we headed, Arch?'

'Nebraska.'

Treber eyed him puzzledly. 'Nebraska?' It was about eighty miles to the Nebraska line, maybe a little more. 'What the hell's Nebraska got, 'side from more dirt farmers than you kin shake a stick at?'

To his surprise, Bowman said, 'You don't like it, Ned, you can always pick a different trail.'

Around them, the other men suddenly paused in their packing. Bristling at Bowman's tone, Treber said stiffly, 'Jus' askin', is all.'

'You'll see,' Bowman replied. 'When I'm good an' ready to tell you, that is.'

So they saddled up and rode north-east and, as the days wore on, Bowman told them they were heading for a town called Freedom Rock. But that was *all* he'd tell them. Behind his back, the boys speculated quietly on what he had in mind. Charlie Breen was convinced it was another bank job. Treber, though, he wasn't so sure. And even now they'd reached their destination, it looked as if Bowman planned to keep them guessing.

All any of them knew for sure was that it must be something big, else why would Bowman have ordered Charlie to cut the telegraph wires earlier that morning, and isolate an already isolated town?

Walt bought himself a ten-cent haircut, then went over to Tom Hardin's general store and killed twenty minutes working his way slowly along every well-stocked shelf. At length he presented the surprised store-keeper with his purchases – a couple cakes of pressed and perfumed soap, a small box of herbal nostrum, an Indian shawl, a bottle of Dr J Bradfield's Female Regulator, a silk reticule, three bunches of spun truck, a book (*Anne* by Constance Fennimore Woolson), two yellowed back-numbers of the *Ladies' Home Journal* and a rose-shaped looking-glass.

Next stop was the Freedom Hotel, a ten-room, two-storey building where he booked two singles, one for himself and one for Ellie – always assuming, of course, that she chose to show up. He handed his purchases – now wrapped neatly in brown paper and waxed string – to the desk-clerk, and gave instructions for the package to be placed in his room.

As he turned and headed for the door, it opened and he stepped aside to allow a dark, rubber-faced man to clump inside. The man, Ace Hotchkiss, looked at him and nodded a greeting. He had very cold, very blue, eyes, Walt noticed, and there was something quietly menacing about him that folks in and around Freedom Rock just weren't used to. He returned the nod, thinking about the man and his four companions, and the way Pat had stiffened when they'd first walked their horses along Main.

Then Hotchkiss brushed by and Walt let himself outside – and all at once the rubber-faced man was forgotten, because the afternoon stage was just beginning its final approach to town.

# THREE

Pat Patterson shifted a ragged stack of circulars from one side of his overcrowded desk to the other, and cursed his lack of organization. Now, if only he'd kept a record of everything the US Marshal's office chose to send him, or filed it in some kind of half-decent fashion that meant he could go straight to the exact sheet of paper he was looking for–

But paperwork had never been his strong-point. And Freedom Rock was such a sleepy little backwater that there'd never been much call to waste time filing endless stacks of nonsense you'd only throw out again three or six months down the line.

Now, though, things were different. The five riders who'd entered town earlier that afternoon had stirred a hazy, worrying kind of memory in him – leastways he thought they did. Something he'd read in passing about two or three weeks before…

He set another stack of circulars down in front of him, glanced at the date in the top right-hand corner and swore. *1884!* That was three years ago! He picked up the stack and dumped it into his wastebasket, then flopped back in his swivel chair and shook his head in despair.

After saying his goodbyes to Walt Canaday, he'd decided to head directly back to his office to hunt up the elusive circular. No sooner had he started to retrace his steps along Main, however, than he'd spotted one of the newcomers – a tall, thin-faced cuss with dark, close-set eyes and a black longhorn moustache – pushing out of the saloon. On impulse he'd changed direction, crossed the street and called, all friendly-like, ''Afternoon, there.'

Glancing at him, and seeing the small brass star he wore on his buttoned vest, the man had slowed down. ''Afternoon,' he'd replied.

'Saw you ride into town jus' now, you an' your friends,' said Pat. 'You boys lookin' for work?'

'Nope. An' before you ask, Marshal, we ain't vagrants, neither.'

'Didn't mean to suggest that you was,' said Pat, placatingly. 'Name's Patterson, by the way, Mr…?'

'Maguire,' said Bowman. It was the first name that came into his head.

'Come a-ways, Mr Maguire?'

'Not far. Julesburg.'

'Plan on stayin' long?'

'Just till we're not here no more,' the man he knew as Maguire replied vaguely. 'You got a reason for askin' so many questions, Marshal?'

'I don't know,' Pat replied honestly. '*Have I?*'

Maguire grinned at him. 'I'd be surprised if you did.'

Pat locked eyes with him for a long, long moment and saw a cool customer from whom he was going to get nothing at all. He sensed danger in this man Maguire too, and that made him regret not going about the town armed.

'Well,' he said, as sociably as he could manage, 'we run a friendly little town here, Maguire. You enjoy your stay, all right? And leave the place as you found it.'

Maguire reached up to touch the brim of his hat and made to move on, but Pat stopped him with another question. 'Hurt yourself, I see.'

Bowman glanced down at his bandaged left hand and lied easily, 'Got a mite careless handlin' some barb-wire. Won't do that again.'

59

'I jus' bet you won't.'

Then the tall man was gone, striding stiffly but confidently along the boardwalk, the tails of his long grey duster – a duster with a noticeable repair on the left side, Pat had noticed, and the remnants of a pale, smudgy discoloration that might have been a washed-out bloodstain – swishing around his long legs.

An injured hand and what might or might not be a bullet hole in the left side of his duster, up around where the man's ribcage would be. Yep, they had all conspired to stir something in his memory, and he quickly continued on his way back to his office, where the great search began.

Now he sat back and tiredly surveyed the room, which was small and dark with an over-large desk, a writing bureau, a file-cabinet and a small, scratched pot-belly stove, all the while trying to remember what he'd done with that last batch of circulars the Marshal's office had sent across from Lincoln. He told himself, *Think, man, think!* – and even as he thought it, his eyes fell to a stack of reports that was sitting on the far edge of the desk and damned if he didn't find himself staring at exactly the one he'd been looking for.

Snatching it up, he read it through as quickly as his limited amount of book-learning would allow. It was a report of a bank robbery in Colfax, Colorado, just over three weeks earlier. Apparently, the manager of the bank had tried to fight off the robbers and wounded or killed one of them before being shot dead himself.

Frowning now, Pat read on, his lips moving silently as he sought to take it all in. A couple of eye-witnesses had claimed that Hobart – he was the bank manager – had shot the boss-outlaw in the hand. Others had said it was a chest-wound.

There'd been five of the bastards all told. Five. And though descriptions were vague, several witnesses had spotted a black man among the group, wearing a cavalry sabre on one hip.

That clinched it. There could no longer be any doubting that these were the same men. All he had to do now was put names to them, figure out what had brought them all the way to Freedom Rock and then…

Swallowing hard, he climbed slowly to his feet, crossed the poky little room on legs like wooden blocks and opened the top drawer of the file cabinet. Carefully he took out a coiled gunbelt with a Remington New

Model Navy .36 in the pocket, and buckled it around his waist.

Then, he thought sickly, all I got to do is arrest them.

The stage – a bright scarlet Concord rocking drunkenly on sturdy leather thoroughbraces – came ploughing along Main Street behind three spans of glistening chestnut horses. Walt stood in the middle of the boardwalk and followed its progress like a man in a dream, hardly able to credit that he was finally reaching the culmination of his eight-month postal courtship.

But, as he gave his ankle jacks one last, quick polish on the backs of his trousers, he reminded himself again that it was still possible that Ellie had decided against making the trip after all, and that she had also lacked the courage to write and tell him so.

His feelings about that were ambivalent. On the one hand, the thought of going back home and picking up his life exactly where he'd left it, was a cheering one. It was the safe option, the one that offered no surprises. On the other, he was surprised at just how disappointed he felt he would be if she really *did* fail to show up.

The stagecoach swayed on along Main, the driver – a short, overweight man in heavily stained jacket and jeans – cracking his long whip high above the heads of the straining team, and hurling insults that were strong enough to blister paint. Bernie Wilkes appeared in the post office doorway, watched the Concord rattle past, its big, bright yellow wheels stirring a dustcloud in its wake, then started walking up towards the Freedom Hotel, where the coach always stopped twice a week.

At last, the driver began to gather in his lines to slow the team, and apply gentle boot-pressure to the long brake-handle. The stage jerked a little, the wheels locked, and then the vehicle came to a slithering kind of halt.

Walt took a step back, his hands bunching anxiously at his sides. The driver turned his lines expertly around the brake-handle and threw him a nod, which he returned. His eyes fixed on the near-side coach-door, just waiting. From where he was standing, he couldn't see inside: it was too dark inside to see much, anyway.

Bernie Wilkes trotted up and called, ''Afternoon, Blake. Makin' good time this afternoon.'

The driver muttered a few words of agreement, took a satchel stencilled with the legend US MAIL from beneath his seat and threw it down. Bernie caught it easily, weighed it in his hands and said, 'Could be whatever you're waitin' for has just arrived, Mr Canaday. You give me thirty minutes to get it all sorted, then come and see.'

Before Walt could reply, the stagecoach door swung open, and for that one, split second, he grew so nervous that he forgot to keep breathing. A moment later, a man in a pale-grey suit climbed down to the board-walk, dusted himself off and went into the hotel, and Walt sighed with such force that his hunched shoulders dropped a good two inches.

In the very next moment, however, the body of the coach leaned a little to one side and a small, white-gloved hand at the end of a slender, green-clad arm reached out to get a steadying grip on the open door. Walt took a pace forward, moving like a man in a dream again, and then, all at once, she was standing there, and he was offering her his right hand.

'Miss Bryant?' he croaked, and had to clear his throat loudly. 'Ellie?'

She looked at him for a long moment, and

then said, 'Walt?'

He laughed nervously. 'Yup.' Then she took his hand and climbed down, and they just looked each other up and down, both blushing and grinning like fools.

Ellie Bryant was tall for a woman, about five feet eight inches, with broad shoulders and a body that tapered, V-like, towards a trim waist before flaring again at the hips. She wore a green taffeta dress with a fashionable black trim, and an embroidered hat from which hung a decorative green ribbon. In her left hand she carried a pierced green fabric parasol.

As they continued looking each other up and down, still grinning and sighing and making awkward little *Well, here we are, then* noises, he saw that she was everything she'd claimed to be. She was in her early thirties, with large green eyes, a pert snub of nose and a small, heart-shaped mouth. Her hair was a deep, luxuriant auburn, and she wore it swept back off her high forehead and gathered together in a silky chignon, or bun.

At last he said, 'Well … I sure am glad to see you.' And he meant it.

'I'm glad to be here,' she replied, her voice soft, pleasant and educated.

'I 'spect it's been quite a journey,' he

noted. In fact, it had been six weeks and some 400 miles.

'It has, yes.'

'I've, ah, I booked you a room at the hotel, here. Figured you might like to rest up awhile.' He dried up then, and they just stared at each other some more. 'I thought I could take you out to my farm tomorrow. You know, so you could take a look around, meet my kids.'

'Yes, I've been looking forward to that.'

'Well then,' said Walt, 'you go on inside, ah, Ellie. Me, I'll get your bags an' be along directly.'

And he told himself with a sudden rush of buoyancy that left him light-headed, Well, I'll be damned! So far so good!

Pat Patterson stood at his small office window, looking out across Main Street to the Freedom Saloon.

It was sunset, and he was a very worried man.

He'd spent the long afternoon going through a stack of reward notices until he found a description that fitted Maguire pretty well.

It gave his real name as Arch Bowman.

After that, it had been relatively easy to

66

search out notices on the men he was said to ride with. The only one who didn't seem to have any paper out on him was the kid with the square face, but Pat figured that was only because he was still so new to the law breaking game that he hadn't yet brought himself to the attention of the authorities.

If the information in each of the other Wanted notices was to be believed, however – and there was no reason for Pat to doubt it – the rest of them were a pretty rough crew.

And it was now his job to arrest them.

He'd thought long and hard about that. Well, it wasn't a chore any sensible man would tackle lightly. At first he'd decided to wire the US Marshal's office in Lincoln and see if they could send him some help, but Bernie Wilkes had told him the line was down. Then he'd tried to convince himself that there was nothing in Freedom Rock for the likes of Bowman and his cronies anyway, and that they were more than likely just passing through. But then he'd stopped by the Freedom Hotel and discovered that the gang had booked themselves a couple of rooms.

They were staying over, then. But why? The obvious answer was that they planned to rob the bank. But there was hardly enough money in the Freedom Rock bank to make a robbery worth the effort.

Anyway, that was beside the point. The point was, Arch Bowman and his associates were wanted by the law and, as a representative of the law, it was his job to arrest them.

Out-classed and all too aware of the fact, he put it off for as long as he could. He watched the sun drop lower and Main Street gradually empty out. One by one, he saw dusty tarpaper windows begin to glow with smoky amber lamplight. He took out his Ingersoll and checked the time. By his reckoning, Bowman and his cronies had now been drinking for something like seven hours. They ought to have taken in just about enough whiskey to dull their wits and slow their gun-hands.

He *hoped*.

At last, he took out his Colt, thumbed back the hammer and turned the cylinder to check the loads. Satisfied that the gun was in good working order, he slid it back into the holster and picked up the Parker shotgun he kept for special occasions, like this one. Thus armed, he went outside, drew himself up and cleared his throat, and when he crossed the street, it was with the slow, shuffling walk of a condemned man.

Worn out by her long journey, Ellie Bryant spent the afternoon resting in the room Walt had booked for her, then freshened up and changed her travelling outfit for a simple plaid skirt and white blouse. The next time Walt saw her, in the foyer of the Freedom Hotel just before sunset, he almost forgot to breathe again.

At his suggestion, they walked along to Vern Crombie's restaurant, which was right next door to the Freedom Saloon. He made no attempt to take her by the arm or offer her his own, and was careful to keep a respectable distance between them at all times.

Over supper, they set about getting to know each other a little better, each of them feeling their way slowly, awkwardly and with elaborate care. He already knew something of her circumstances, of course: that she was the youngest of seven daughters, to whom had fallen the unenviable duty of nursing an elderly, widowed and ailing mother at the expense of her own life, and with the obvious consequence – that when Mrs Bryant had finally passed away about a year earlier, Ellie found herself largely friendless and, at the age of thirty-one, woefully inexperienced in the ways of the world. Wanting to escape from St Cloud and start life afresh, she'd signed on with a matrimonial agency in Sioux Falls, Dakota, where she had eventually received a postal introduction to Walt.

Over time, she had learned something of Walt's history, too: of how Kate had miscarried two years earlier and died, weak and bloodless, for want of proper medical attention. In his long, painstakingly written letters, he'd told her all about his life, the farm, his children, the town and its inhabitants, and when they got to know and trust each other a little more, they'd discussed the burden of loneliness too, and the basic need for man to have a mate. As tactfully as she'd known how, Ellie had suggested that perhaps he was really seeking a replacement mother for his children, but he'd assured her that, while that was true up to a point, he also hoped to find a partner for himself, too.

Now, as they nursed their after-supper coffees, Ellie looked through the restaurant window at the darkening town beyond and remarked, smilingly, 'It's exactly how I pictured it, Walt. You have a gift for description.'

He looked out too, saw Pat Patterson crossing the street with a shotgun in his fists and frowned briefly.

'Walt?'

Looking back at her, he answered a little distantly, 'Well, I, ah, don't know about that, but I *will* wager it's a mite different to what you've been used to in Minnesota.'

Pat climbed onto the boardwalk and walked right past, looking neither left nor right but straight ahead, and Walt suddenly began to feel strangely anxious, somehow: restless, like something bad was just about to happen.

Then Ellie was speaking again. 'Have you, ah, told your children much about me, Walt?'

'Oh, uh, a little.'

'And how do they feel about, ah, having a woman about the place? I ask because – well, it's important to me that they know I'm not here to take the place of their mother.'

'I reckon they know that well enough,' he replied. 'I mean, no one expects you to take Kate's place.'

'Not that I'd object, you understand,' she said hurriedly. 'I'd like them to feel that they

71

could trust me, come to me with any of their little worries, just as they could their real mother. But I wouldn't just expect it. I know I have to earn their trust.' That said, she suddenly felt a little less apprehensive, indeed, almost expansive. 'You know,' she went on, 'I'm not the kind of person to make snap judgements, but I do like it here. After St Cloud, it's so peaceful and unhurried.'

'It is, that,' he allowed.

Looking him right in the face, she said confidentially, and with a blush, 'If this ... you know, our arrangement ... if it doesn't work out, it won't be for want of trying.'

He gave her a self-conscious, quirky little smile and opened his mouth to make some sort of reply – but before he could say a word, Freedom Rock suddenly trembled with a wild flurry of gunfire.

Pat had stood awhile outside the saloon, just looking in to get the positions of Bowman and his men fixed firmly in his mind. They were all occupying a table in the far right-hand corner, each man sitting with his back to the wall and facing the batwings. Bowman's gun hand, he noticed, was hidden beneath the table. He made a mental note to watch that.

Then, grimly, he shoved inside.

Business in the Freedom was about as poor now as it had been all day. Regularly spaced, guttering lanterns threw butter-coloured light down over a couple of townsmen shooting the breeze up at the bar, and a few more who were playing cards for matches at one of the scratched tables. Cigarette smoke drifted lazily around the rafters, most of it coming from a grubby old rumpot named Joe Banks, who played Len's piano, badly, in return for drinks.

From the corner of his eye, Pat saw Len Parsons shove himself up off the bar and look curiously in his direction, but he ignored the man. His attention was fixed on the five outlaws at the corner table: he was watching them very closely, just waiting for them to make a move against him. But they never even glanced in his direction.

Pat strode through the room, the shotgun held slantwise across his chest, and sensing that something was about to happen, the conversation at the bar suddenly dried up, the card-players stopped playing, and Joe Banks hit a couple of bum notes and then abandoned the yellowed ivories altogether. All at once, the only sounds were Pat's heavy footsteps and the low murmur of conversation coming from the corner table.

At last Pat planted himself in front of the table and said, 'Bowman?'

The low conversation stopped, and Bowman, previously known as Maguire, looked up at him, his close-set, dark eyes narrowing faintly. Pat returned his stare as levelly as he could manage, and allowed his own blue eyes to rake along the line to take in Treber and Craven, Hotchkiss and Breen.

Then he said, 'Get your hands up, the lot of you. You're under arrest.'

Bowman's only response was a slow, chilly sneer that made his thick moustache stir sluggishly, like a well-fed black snake. 'You don't say,' he replied, and Charlie Breen flicked ash off his Cross Cut cigarette and giggled.

'I *do* say,' said Pat, dry-mouthed. 'Now get your hands up, all of you, an' no sudden moves, 'cause by God you'll regret it. An' you, Bowman, you get your gun hand up here where I can see it.'

'What's the charge, Marshal?' asked Treber.

Glancing at him, Pat said, 'Well, we'll start with that bank job you boys pulled down in–'

He realized then that he'd allowed himself to be distracted – that he'd given Bowman exactly the chance he'd been waiting for.

Suddenly the room rocked to the sound of a single, throaty gunblast, and a splintery hole punched up through the table just in front of Bowman. The bullet that made it travelled on, hit Pat in the sternum and pushed him backwards. His face went slack with surprise, his eyes widened in disbelief, and without meaning to, his finger tightened on the shotgun's trigger and the weapon discharged itself into the ceiling.

As plaster fell in a miniature blizzard, Bowman came up onto his feet, his chair, sliding backwards, away from his straightening legs, and with his bandaged hand he fanned the Frontier model Colt .44 he'd been holding all this time, and three more bullets punched a line across Pat's chest.

Pat jerked, twitched and cried out as each small, red hole burst across his buttoned buckskin vest, one, two, three … and, as he continued to lurch backwards under the impacts, the last sound he ever heard was Charlie Breen, giggling.

Already edgy, Walt leapt up as soon as he heard the gunfire, and fixing Ellie with a hard stare, he snapped, 'Stay here!'

He quit the restaurant at a run, not sure what he intended to do but knowing he had to do *something*, because Pat Patterson was a friend, and unless he was much mistaken, it was Pat who needed help right now.

He burst out onto the boardwalk, turned and ran wildly along to the saloon just as the batwings pushed open. He drew up short as Pat staggered outside, the shotgun still grasped tightly in his right fist. He moved slowly, without even being aware of it, without even being aware of who he was or why he was still standing when, by rights, he should be down and dying.

In the faint street-light, Walt saw that Pat's vest and shirt were black with spilled blood, and his face twisted and a low sound of pain fell from his lips. He called, dumbly, 'Pat...?'

Then Pat dropped the shotgun and fell forward, into his arms, and Walt caught him, stumbled a bit beneath his weight. He said it again. 'Pat...?' And then Pat just slid through his arms and Walt went down with him, lowering him to the boardwalk as gently as he could, still not understanding, still not comprehending.

He knelt beside his friend and watched the

life drain out of him.

'P-Pat...?'

Pat was dead.

For a long moment then there were no other sounds, and no other movement. He stared down at Pat and started trembling. Then the heavy clatter of boots broke the silence; the batwings shoved outward with a sharp, intrusive squeak, and shadows splashed across the body.

Walt looked up into Bowman's face, into his eyes. To one side of the man stood the hardcases with whom he'd ridden into town earlier, and they all just returned his stare with flat, cold stares of their own. He thought again about the way Pat had stiffened at first sight of them and wanted to control his trembling but couldn't. His gaze dropped to the .44 in Bowman's hand; smoke still drifted from the long barrel.

Gradually he became aware of other shadows falling around him. Craning his neck he recognized Bill Summerfield, Bernie Wilkes, Les Parsons, Joe Banks and others, saw his own shock mirrored in their wide eyes and open mouths. And at last he looked back at Bowman and said, hoarsely, 'You killed him.'

Bowman's lipless mouth worked in a

short, smug tic, like he was proud of the fact.

'You *killed* him!'

'An' you'll be next iffen you don't get outa my road,' Bowman replied at last.

Still stunned, Walt looked again at Pat, with his pale face and staring eyes and bullet-riddled chest covered in blood. He caught sight of the shotgun lying beside him and wanted to snatch it up and use it on Pat's murderer. The muscles in his shoulders tensed, and for one crazy moment he was actually going to do it. But then Bowman snarled, 'Don't,' and the madness left him. He looked up at the man, shaking his head in bafflement, still unable to believe that something like this could have happened, on this of all days...

More townsfolk were gathering, though they were being careful to keep their distance. Walt turned his head and saw Ellie standing among them, her face white, like that of a ghost; and seeing her made him remember his children. They'd already lost their mother: if they lost their father as well...

Slowly, like an old, old man, he straightened to his full height and meekly stepped aside, his shoulders slack, his head bowed.

Charlie Breen giggled at him, and then he, Bowman and all the others pushed past, stepped over the body and swaggered up towards the Freedom Hotel.

# FOUR

With no facilities to speak of for preserving the dead beyond a few days, especially in summer, Pat Patterson was buried early the following morning, in the drab little cemetery just north-west of town. Pat's elderly, widowed mother – all the family he had – and most of Freedom Rock's modest population turned out to pay their respects. So too did Ellie.

Wanting to spare her feelings as much as possible, Walt had told her that there was no need for her to attend if she didn't want to, but in that quiet, cultured way of hers, she'd insisted. And now, as they all clustered around the open grave and Pastor Fleming read the lesson, Walt became aware of a weird, cloying kind of silence among the mourners. Like himself, folks still couldn't believe that the events of the previous evening had really happened. It just didn't seem possible that Pat could have been shot dead.

But he *had* been shot dead. And, Walt reminded himself wretchedly, on the very day that Ellie had come to town.

As they bowed their heads in prayer, he threw a quick, guarded glance at her profile and wondered what was going through her mind right at that moment. Compassion for the man who had just lost his life in the line of duty, certainly ... but also, more than likely, the first nagging doubts about whether or not she'd done the right thing in coming all this way to start a new life in a land where they still shot men down in the street.

Walt hadn't trusted himself to say much when he'd rejoined her outside the restaurant immediately after the shooting. All he'd done was take her by the arm and lead her slowly away from the growing crowd. At first, neither of them had really known what to say to the other. Then Ellie had asked in a hesitant whisper, 'Did you know him very well, Walt? The dead man?'

His response was a quick, nervy kind of shrug. 'Him and me, we both set our caps for Kate when we was just kids,' he explained self-consciously. 'He tried every trick in the book to make her choose him over me, and I guess I was just as bad.'

'She must have been a very special woman.'

'She was.'

'You were rivals, then?'

'That makes it sound like we was enemies,' he replied. 'And we was never that.' He fell silent, swallowed hard and kept looking straight ahead, into the dark middle distance. 'When Kate ... when she died, Pat was ... well, he took the loss almost as bad as me. I guess each of us helped the other to get over it.'

'Does he have a wife now?'

He shook his head. 'He told me once, he said ... said as how I'd won the only woman he was ever likely to care for.' And now, he added silently, they're gone, the both of them: Kate and Pat.

'I'm so sorry, Walt,' she said helplessly. 'Truly I am.'

'Me too, Ellie. Sorry it had to happen, an' sorry you had to see it.'

With a start, he came back to the present, realized that the rough plank coffin had been lowered into the ground and that folks had started drifting away, women dabbing at their eyes and noses, men shaking their heads grimly and allowing as how this never should've happened in the first place. A small group of townsmen had gathered nearby and were conversing animatedly in low tones. After a while they came over, doffing their hats or touching the brims to Ellie.

'Miz Bryant?' said Bill Summerfield, reaching out to take Ellie's hand by the fingertips. 'Pleased to make your acquaint'nce, ma'am. Heard a lot about you from Walt here, all of it, ah, good.' The men behind him nodded in sober agreement. 'Like to have a word with Walt alone, iffen you'd, uh, excuse us for a moment.'

She glanced briefly at Walt, said, 'Of course,' then turned and wandered away, gathering the black lace shawl she'd worn as a mark of respect tighter around her shoulders, even though the morning was now warming up fast.

'Walt,' Bill said urgently. 'Few of us been talkin'. Them sonsabitches who gunned Pat, we can't jus' let 'em get away with it. We figger we got to arrest 'em.'

'That's what Pat was fixin' to do when they killed him,' explained Len Parsons. 'Bernie here went an' took a look around his office early this mornin', found four Wanted notices spread across his desk. Them fellers … they're outlaws, man! Bank an' road agents.'

Walt kept his eyes on Bill. 'We'?' he repeated.

Bill and a few of the other men nodded again, and Bernie Wilkes offered conspiratorially. 'The line's down, Walt, otherwise we could send for help. As it stands, we figure we're on our own in this.'

'What we want to know now,' said Bill, 'is – are you with us?'

'What's the plan?'

Bill stared back at him in something like surprise. Clearly, he and the others hadn't thought that far ahead yet. Tom Hardin, a tired-looking man with grey hair and a lined face, said, 'We just thought we'd arrest 'em. You know, arm ourselves an' go brace 'em.'

'An' you think they'd let you do that?'

'They can't fight *all* of us.'

Walt shook his head, remembering the coldness he'd seen in Bowman's eyes the night before, the man's willingness to kill. 'They'll gun down anyone who goes against 'em,' he said. 'Christ, they've already proved that.'

'You sayin' you're not with us, then?' Bill muttered frostily.

'I'm sayin' that, happen we try bracin' them fellers like you say, some of us, maybe *all* of us, gonna end up like Pat.' He shook his head. 'That's not a risk I can take, fellers. I got three younkers to consider, not to

85

mention my intended.'

'Ah, sure,' said Vern Crombie, his voice shot through with disgust. 'You jus' go on about your life, Walt. Don't you worry none 'bout what them fellers did to Pat.'

Walt's slightly sad mouth thinned out as his normally even temper slipped a notch. 'You think I don't want 'em to pay for what they did, Vern? Is that it?'

'That's not it at all, Walt,' Bernie Wilkes said hurriedly. 'We jus' feel ... well, we've got to do somethin'.'

'Well, gettin' yourselves wounded or worse isn't it,' Walt replied, harder than he meant to. He ranged his eyes over them, and they shifted uncomfortably beneath his stare. A liveryman, a storekeeper, a Western Union clerk, a saloon-owner, the guy who fried grits at the local eaterie – what could they hope to do against professional badmen? 'I don't like it any more'n you do,' he said hoarsely. 'But that's jus' the way it is. I got kin to consider, an' so have you. If you got any sense, one of you'll ride for Julesburg.' It was the nearest town of any size or consequence, about fifty miles north. 'You can wire the US Marshal's office from there, let them handle it.'

'An' in the meantime?' asked Tom Hardin.

Walt shrugged. 'Rest of you sit tight,' he said firmly. 'An' hope like hell they don't make any more trouble.'

When he got back to his office, Russell Drake, the forty-six year-old editor of the Freedom Rock *Dispatch,* found Bowman waiting for him.

Short and thick-set, with a round, friendly face and a thin scraping of mouse-brown hair combed left-to-right across an otherwise bald dome, Drake had gone up to the cemetery to pay his last respects to Pat Patterson, and on the slow, thoughtful walk back to town, had started to compose the beginnings of a fitting tribute to the marshal in his head. He planned to make much of Pat's sense of duty, his honesty and humour and willingness to help others. But more than that, he intended to vilify the gun-swift scum who'd killed him. Bernie Wilkes had furnished him with their names – well, four of them, at least. Now, he saw it as his duty to publish a blistering editorial telling them that sooner or later, they would all suffer the consequences of their evil ways. He intended to entitle his editorial, 'The Good Lord Pays Debts Without Money'.

A newspaperman practically all his adult

life, Drake was a firm believer in the power of the Press – even the small-circulation, once-a-fortnight, local Press in which he himself worked. If he could inspire the people of Freedom Rock to make a stand against this man Bowman and his cronies, they would soon go in search of easier pickings elsewhere. But if he said nothing, if the townsfolk did nothing, they would stay and exploit what they rightly perceived as weakness for all it was worth – and that, he simply could not allow. Last night it had been Pat Patterson. Who might it be this afternoon, or tonight, or tomorrow?

Still deep in thought, he crossed Main and dug a hand into the pocket of his dusty black suit pants, searching for the office key. And just as he stepped up onto the opposite boardwalk, he saw Bowman waiting for him down at the far end, a tall silhouette with broad shoulders, long legs and a wide-brimmed hat, standing hip-shot and insolent, completely and utterly sure of himself.

Drake immediately slowed to a more cautious pace, all thought of his powerful editorial temporarily forgotten. Instead, he asked himself what possible business the outlaw could have with him. Nothing came to mind, so he continued on up to the office, which was housed in a long, narrow clapboard building with a plate-glass window upon which the name of the newspaper had been painted in gold. Bowman watched him come through narrowed eyes, his thumbs hooked behind the cartridge belt around his lean waist, forearms hitching back the folds of his long grey duster.

When he was still about five or six feet away from the man, Drake came to a halt, and Bowman, seeing only a stocky, overweight pen-pusher in a dusty black suit and muley hat, looked down at him with something like contempt.

'Help you?' Drake asked coldly.

'Could be,' allowed Bowman.

He held Bowman's stare with his own dark, honest eyes for a moment longer. Then, when it became obvious that the outlaw wasn't going to volunteer any further information, he unlocked the door and pushed it open to reveal the cluttered mess beyond. Rolls of newsprint and pots of printer's ink were stacked everywhere: a low shelf to his left was piled high with old, yellowing copies of the *Dispatch*, and behind the single, large desk in the centre of the boarded floor stood a composing table and a huge black slab of iron levers, rollers and boards that was his proudest possession – a Babcock steam-driven printing press.

Bowman followed him inside, flexing his stiff, bandaged left hand as he glanced around.

'All right, Mr Bowman,' said Drake, sweeping off his hat and moving round behind the desk to flop into the swivel chair there. 'What can I do for you?'

Showing no surprise that Drake should know his real name, Bowman said, 'You lived in these parts long, mister?'

'A few years. Why?'

'You keep back numbers of your paper?'

'What is it you're looking for?'

Ignoring the question, Bowman went over to the low shelf, scooped up a stack of back numbers and started going through them quickly, checking the dates. 'How far back do you keep these things?' he demanded without looking up.

'The *Dispatch*'s been going for fifteen years,' Drake replied, opening a drawer and reaching inside. 'I've been the owner-editor for the last three.'

'That's not what I asked.'

'No,' agreed Drake, bringing out a .38-calibre New Line Police Colt. 'Now put your hands up, you damned butcher.'

He'd done it all so smoothly that Bowman hadn't even seen it coming. Now, stiffening at the sudden hardening of Drake's tone, he slowly raised his head from the back numbers he'd been checking through, glanced around, saw the gun and stood a little straighter. 'What the hell you playin' at, newspaperman?'

'It's called citizens' arrest,' Drake replied, and stood up again. 'Now, get your hands up, Bowman. Pat Patterson was a good man, and as God's my witness, you're going to pay for killing him.'

Regaining his composure, Bowman only offered him a wolfish kind of snarl-grin. 'Put that gun away afore you hurt yourself,' he rasped. 'Dammit, I been braced by tougher men than you an' lived to tell the tale.'

'Not this time,' Drake answered, his voice tight, low, and just a little scared. 'Like it or not, you're under arrest, Bowman. I'm taking you down to the jailhouse and locking you behind bars, and if your friends want to bust you out, they'll be welcome to try. But the minute they do, I'll put a bullet through your skull and to hell with the consequences.'

Bowman's grin widened a little. 'You know

somethin'?' he asked. 'You got sand, mister. I like that in a man. But you ain't takin' me *anywhere.*'

'I wouldn't be any too sure of that, was I you. Now, for the last time, get your hands up!'

Even before he'd finished speaking, Bowman flared into action, throwing the stack of papers at him and quickly dodging to one side. Reacting instinctively, Drake flinched, his eyes closed for perhaps two seconds, no longer. At the same time he swung his left arm out to swat the newspapers aside, he pulled the trigger and the handgun barked and jumped in his fist.

The gunblast filled the room, punched through the plate-glass window and the whole thing caved in on itself and then fell outwards, showering the boardwalk with splintery, gold-painted shards.

By that time, Bowman had closed the gap between them.

Rearing up right beside him, he plucked the gun out of Drake's fist and tossed it aside, then grabbed Drake by one lapel and hit him a short, sharp punch right in the face. Drake squealed, having never experienced pain like it before, and Bowman hit him again, and again, and again, short, savage little jabs that mashed his lips and broke his nose.

How long that pummelling lasted, Drake had no idea. But when he tired of it, Bowman thrust the newspaperman away from him and he fell backwards, over the swivel chair, bleeding from one nostril and several splits in his swelling lips. He landed hard on the floor and tried to pick himself up, but Bowman, still towering above him, kicked him viciously in the side.

Drake felt at least one of his ribs break with a wet snap. He hunched up under the impact of the blow, groaned and mumbled, 'No more … pu-please…'

But he was going to get more, whether he wanted it or not.

Bowman twisted his bandaged left hand into Drake's collar, hauled him back to his feet and punched him hard in the stomach. The air left Drake in a rush and he sagged, but Bowman didn't let him fall, he held him there and belly-punched him again. He turned his attention back to Drake's face after that, sent him reeling across the office with a right cross, another, another, using the right again and again in order to spare the wounded-and-healing left. Drake slammed hard against the printing press, bounced off and dropped to his hands and knees, wheezing like a bellows, shaking his head sluggishly, blood hanging in thick red strings from his ruined mouth, teeth slanting this way and that in his bloody gums.

'N … no more … *please…*' he husked, weeping softly.

Bowman kicked him one last time, then dropped to a crouch beside him. 'You gonna help me, now?' he growled, digging Drake in the shoulder. 'Huh?'

Drake nodded and said, through ruined lips, 'Wh … what is it you want to … know?'

Bowman told him … and it was the very last thing Drake had expected to hear.

With the funeral over and done with, Walt escorted Ellie back to the hotel, excused himself and went to hitch up the wagon. He worked quickly, anxious to get Ellie out of town and away from any further unpleasantness as soon as possible.

He very nearly made it, too.

The town was just falling behind them when Russell Drake's single, wild gunshot crackled through the warm, mid-morning air and made him bring the wagon to a creaky stop. Seated side by side on the high seat, Walt and Ellie twisted around to look back at the sun-dried cluster of plank-built dwellings standing either side of the deserted street, and knowing nothing of Bowman's visit to the *Dispatch* office, Walt wondered if Bill and the others had gone ahead and tried to arrest the outlaw and his companions after all.

He dearly hoped not.

After a moment, he felt Ellie's eyes on him, guessed the question in her mind and shook his head. He had no real idea what the gunshot signified, if indeed it signified anything at all. Maybe Bowman was shooting at cockroaches in his hotel room. Maybe Bill Summerfield had gone and shot himself in the foot. Had he been alone, had he not had Ellie and his kids to consider, he might have turned the rig around and gone back to find out. As it was, he slapped the reins across his horses' hindquarters and kept them headed south, and he hated himself for refusing to get involved.

Morning pushed towards noon, and the box wagon trundled on through empty hills and rolling plains. They travelled mostly in silence, until Walt noticed that Ellie was growing increasingly restive beside him.

'You all right?' he asked.

She nodded, but her expression remained

faintly troubled.

'You sure?' he pursued. 'Is it this heat?'

This time she shook her head and glanced around. 'No. It's just … I had no idea this country was quite so … well, *big*. Or that your farm was quite so far from town.' She offered him a brief, self-conscious, uneasy sort of laugh. 'I'm just not used to so much space, I suppose. It's silly, I know, but I actually find it a little … intimidating.'

'It's a big land, right enough,' he allowed, trying to keep his voice light and casual while he told himself miserably, she hates it. She hates it because it's nothing like St Cloud.

Noon came and went. The wagon rattled on until, at length, they crested a grassy ridge and saw the farm spread out below them. Walt hauled back on the reins, brought the team to a halt and said, proudly, 'Well, there it is, Ellie.' And after a moment's hesitation, he added cautiously, *'Home.'*

He watched as her large green eyes traced the orderly lines of winter wheat, maize and sugar beet, then moved to take in the yard and the buildings he'd erected around it, but to his dismay she made no comment one way or the other about what she saw there.

Squaring his shoulders again, forcing himself to remain optimistic, he clucked the horses back to a walk and by the time he wheeled the wagon into the yard, Matt, Joey and Sam had come out onto the porch to greet them. As he stepped on the brake lever, Walt saw that Matt had made them all dress in their best Sunday-go-to-meeting clothes, clearly as anxious to make a good impression as he was himself.

Jumping down, he hurried around the wagon to help Ellie descend from the high seat. There was a long, uncomfortable silence as she set one dainty foot awkwardly on the wheel-hub, then allowed him to put his hands around her waist and lift her down. 'Ellie,' he said, as she dusted herself down and fidgeted a little with her hair, 'these here are my younkers.'

'Pleased to know you, Miss Bryant,' said Matt, with a wary nod.

'Oh, please, call me Ellie. All of you.'

Glancing up at his brother and sister, Sam stepped forward and offered her his right hand. 'How do,' he said gravely.

Ellie frowned at him, for his colouring – red hair and quite remarkable violet-blue eyes – was entirely different to that of his brother and sister. Then she shook hands with him and said with a smile, 'You must be young Samuel.'

'Sam,' he corrected at once.

'Sam, yes,' she agreed, the smile faltering a little. 'Your father has told me all about you. About all of you.'

Ignoring Ellie, Joey fixed Walt with a hard stare and said accusingly, 'You said you'd be home early, you promised.'

Walt's face clouded momentarily. 'Somethin' happened,' he replied vaguely. 'We got delayed. But we're here now, so why don't you all get on inside while I unhitch the team? I daresay you could stand some coffee an' cake before I show you round the place, huh, Ellie?'

As he hopped back onto the wagon and turned it towards the shed, Matt, Joey and Sam all stood to one side so that Ellie could go into the house ahead of them. Inside, she threw a quick, curious glance around, saw a spindle-backed settle before the fireplace, a slat-backed rocker and a ten-plate stove that stood three feet tall and eighteen inches wide.

'You can sit down, if you like,' invited Sam. But when she made to sit in the rocker, Joey said sharply, 'Not there!' And then, quieter, 'That was Momma's chair.'

For one long, awkward moment Ellie just stood there, unsure what to do. Then Matt cleared his throat and said, 'The settle's more comfortable anyway, ma'am.'

He herded his brother and sister through to the kitchen, Joey glancing back over one shoulder with what Ellie could only interpret as open hostility, and when Walt came through the door ten minutes later, he found her still standing, but bent slightly forward at the waist to inspect a small, sepia-coloured tintype in a frame on the mantelpiece.

'Your wife?' she asked as he came to stand beside her.

He picked up the frame and murmured, 'Uh-huh.'

'She was beautiful.'

'That she was,' he replied almost reverently. As she looked at him and saw the way he looked at the woman in the tintype, she suddenly realized that, no matter what she did to make this man and his children happy, no matter how hard she tried to adapt to life in this wild and lonely land, she would never be more than a replacement for Kate Canaday – and a poor one, at that.

It was a sad, demoralizing little thought.

Things got a little better as the afternoon wore on, but only just.

Walt, Matt and Sam worked hard to mind their manners in front of her, but every time she glanced at Joey, she found the girl scowling at her. It was obvious that, as far as she was concerned, no-one was ever going to take the place of her mother.

Still, Ellie tried not to let the girl's attitude upset her. After all, she had been under no illusions about the difficult task she had taken on. Walt's children were bound to be wary of her at first. That was only to be expected. But she was fully prepared to earn their trust, and hardly expected to win them over in a matter of hours.

So she listened politely as Walt told her all about the farm, the hogs, the hens, their neighbours, and eventually the children grew bored and asked permission to go off and tend their chores, leaving Walt to suggest that he show her around the place.

As they wandered along side by side, Walt still keeping a seemly distance between them at all times, he told her all about the water he'd piped through to the kitchen and out back and pointed out their real glass windows with a sense of eagerness and pride that was almost pathetic. He was trying so hard to impress her that she actually felt sorry for him, for his position was probably no easier than her own. But that wave of sympathy only darkened her mood, because she wanted to feel *love* for him, not sorrow.

At last his guided tour came to an end and he gestured that she should take one of the chairs on the porch, remarking wistfully, 'Kate an' me, we often used to sit here an' just watch the sun go down.'

Kate again, she thought a little testily, and immediately felt guilty. In the next moment, spotting Sam scattering dried corn for some strutting hens on the other side of the yard, she said, 'He's a very polite little fellow. But where does he get his colouring from, Walt?'

'His mother,' he replied.

She frowned. 'I thought that Kate—'

'He's adopted,' he explained.

'Oh.'

'Uh-huh. 'Bout nine years ago – nine years next winter – I found him an' his momma hock-deep in snow, right up there on yonder slope.'

She followed his line of vision, interested and trying to visualize what he was telling her. 'Looked like they'd been travellin' hard when the weather closed in on 'em,' he continued matter-of-factly. 'The woman's horse must've lost its footing, spilled her an' the baby into the snow an' then snapped a foreleg.'

And for just a moment then he was back there, fighting his way through that mad, noisy blizzard with the temperature somewhere around forty below and the wind shoving at him so hard that he fell and had to claw back to his booted feet more times than he could count. But still he'd pushed on, not really believing the evidence of his eyes, a tall, lean man bundled into a thick sheepskin jacket, his hat tied on with a scarf, his hands stuffed into fur-lined gloves, wading through settled and still-falling snow, eyelids flickering as the howling blast spat ice-flakes at him. Stumbling, slipping, righting himself and climbing ever higher towards the dead body of the horse and the woman huddled unconscious, or worse, beside it.

It was only then, as he dropped to his knees beside her, reached out and turned her gently onto her back, that he saw the baby she was hugging to herself – a baby that was wailing plaintively, flexing tiny wet hands and squirming in her arms...

'What happened?' Ellie asked softly.

Her voice brought him back to the present. 'They was both nearer dead than alive,' he replied, speaking almost to himself now. 'An' the woman, she did die later that night, though me an' Kate fought like the dickens to save her. But young Sam there, somehow he pulled through, an' we adopted him.'

'Just like that?'

'Well, it wasn't as simple as I made it sound. I mean, we made enquiries after his blood kin first, had to, but we didn't have much to go on. The woman, she wasn't local, no one'd ever seen her in these parts before, an' neither was she carryin' anythin' to say who she was, where she was from or where she was headed. Pat Patterson circulated the story up an' down the line, but if she had any family or friends, they never came forward to claim the boy.'

'So you and Kate took him for your own.'

'Uh-huh,' he said again. 'An' I ain't never regretted it.'

# FIVE

About thirty minutes later, Ellie glanced up at the westering sun and said she'd best be headed back to town.

Right away, Walt's face clouded and he said quietly, 'Reckon I'd feel a sight happier if you was to stay out here with us, Ellie. Least until Bowman an' his partners move on.'

But she shook her head and reminded him gently, 'We had this conversation before we left town this morning, Walt. And I stand by what I told you then: it simply wouldn't do for me to stay out here, unchaperoned. People would talk.'

He *pshawed*. 'Not *these* people.'

'I'm sorry, Walt,' she said a little firmer. 'I really can't stay.'

He looked pained. 'If it's a question of trust,' he began awkwardly, 'I give you my word that—'

'It's not a question of trust,' she cut in. 'It's more a question of … space.' And looking directly into his eyes, she explained, 'I need time to think.'

He sifted the implications of that for a long moment, then said hesitantly, 'About … us.'

'It's not that I don't like you, Walt,' she replied uncomfortably. 'I have nothing against you, or your children, or the farm, or even the town. But it's all so *different* to what I've been used to, what I imagined. Maybe *too* different.' She rose to her feet and brushed down her plaid skirt. 'It's a big step we're thinking of taking,' she continued quietly. 'I want to make sure it's the right one, for both of us.'

Nodding, he said in a flat voice, 'Sure.' And excusing himself, he went to hitch up the team for the long haul back to Freedom Rock.

As he set to work, he considered what she'd said. He couldn't really blame her for having second thoughts. After all, it wasn't much of a life he was offering her, just three kids, a farm and not much of anything else. As she herself had said, the reality of it all had proved to be completely different to what she'd been expecting. And the violence she'd witnessed the previous night, as well as the isolation she'd felt on the way out here this morning, had done little to help matters.

He shook his head. Nope. She'd told him she wanted time to think, but what she really meant was that she'd already reached her decision, and just wanted to find the best and kindest way to let him know it.

Well, he might be slow, but he wasn't stupid. She didn't need to find a way to tell him, because he'd already worked it out for himself.

She just didn't want this kind of life, after all.

'Is she going, now?'

He'd been so deep in thought that the question made him start. Turning, he saw Joey lingering in the wagon-shed doorway and said, 'If you mean Ellie … yeah, she's goin' now.'

'Good,' said the girl.

'You just show her some respect, Miss Josephine,' he said sharply.

'Why should I?' the girl countered defiantly. 'I don't like her.'

'You don't *know* her.'

'I know she'll never be my momma.'

The fire went out of his eyes when she said that, and he allowed softly, 'No. No, she won't be.'

A short time later he led the team back out into the yard. On the shaded porch, Ellie was saying her goodbyes to Matt and Sam. When he brought the wagon to a halt in front of them, Sam said eagerly, 'Can we go to town, too, Pa?'

He hesitated before replying. He didn't really want to take the kids into Freedom Rock right now, for the same reason that he wanted Ellie to stay out here, but they'd already been alone for one night, and would be alone for much of the coming evening if he didn't let them tag along.

With a shrug, he said, 'Long as Ellie here doesn't mind.'

'Not at all,' she replied.

Sam let loose a cheer and hopped up and down, his antics breaking some of the tension between the two adults, and ten minutes later the wagon rattled north with Walt and Ellie sharing the high seat in silence and Matt, Joey and Sam kneeling in the flat bed behind.

The journey back to Freedom Rock didn't seem quite as long as the journey out, and it was just a little past seven o'clock when they rolled onto Main Street. Walt eyed the town bleakly, wondering what, if anything, had happened in his absence. The boardwalks were largely empty, the town quiet but for the off-key piano-playing of Joe Banks down at the Freedom Saloon.

He brought the wagon to a halt alongside Bill Summerfield's livery stable, looped the lines around the brake handle and climbed down. Behind him, Matt, Joey and Sam leapt from the flat bed, still blissfully unaware of Pat Patterson's death and just excited to be in town. As he helped Ellie down, Walt said, 'You kids stay close by, now, an' don't wander. I'll be back soon as I've seen Ellie down to the hotel.'

Sam's face dropped. 'Can't we go down to Mr Hardin's?' he asked.

Ruffling the boy's hair, Walt explained to Ellie, 'If this young man's got one weakness in life, it's strap candy. But not just *any* strap candy. Tom Hardin sells a special one, doesn't he, son?'

Sam nodded eagerly, his violet-blue eyes saucering. 'It's all the colours of the rainbow,' he told Ellie.

Matching his enthusiasm, she said, 'It sounds delicious! Would you mind if I bought him some, Walt? You've been so kind to me that I'd like to treat all of you.'

'No call for that,' said Walt, and beside him, Joey muttered truculently, 'I don't want anything, anyway.'

'I'd like to,' said Ellie, pretending that she

109

hadn't heard the girl.

Walt sighed. Well, they couldn't get into much trouble down at Tom Hardin's, and while they were thus occupied, he could seek out Bill Summerfield and find out whether or not Bowman had made any more trouble in town. 'All right,' he said. 'But you kids, you behave yourselves, now.'

Sam gave another cheer and Ellie stepped up onto the boardwalk with Matt and Sam flanking her and Joey shuffling along in her wake.

Walt watched them go for a moment, then went into the dusk-filled stable. 'Bill?'

He heard a movement in the small office at the back of the place, and a moment later Bill Summerfield poked his head around the doorframe. He squinted through the growing gloom until he identified Walt's long silhouette, then came forward in a hurry.

'Walt!' he hissed. 'What the hell are you doing back in town? I was just fixin' to ride out to your place!'

Walt frowned at him, the smaller man's obvious agitation immediately putting him on his guard. 'What's happened?' he asked.

'It's Bowman, Walt. He's been askin' questions.'

Not understanding him, Walt said, 'What

kind of questions?' And then, more urgently, 'Somethin' to do with the bank? Is that it?'

Bill shook his head. 'Questions 'bout a red-headed woman who passed through here nine years ago,' he replied gravely, adding, 'And the baby she was carryin' with her at the time.'

'K-kidnap?' Ed Craven stammered in disbelief. 'Is that why we c-come all this way, Arch? To k-kidnap some snot-nosed younker?'

Bowman threw him a quick, dangerous glance. 'Not just *any* younker,' he said softly. 'My *son.*'

All at once the air inside the faded little hotel room was charged with new interest. Ned Treber, who had previously considered himself Bowman's closest confederate, slowly straightened up in the ladderback chair he'd been occupying in the corner, causing his sabre to scrape quietly against the thin carpet. So, he thought, this is what it's all about, and carefully remarked, 'Di'n't even know you wuz married, Arch.'

There was no good reason why Treber, or any of them, should. It had happened a long time before their trails had crossed – and even then, Bowman had only been married for about a year. Just long enough to produce a son, to spurn the love of a good, decent woman and give her no choice but to run out on him.

'Well,' he returned in a rasp, 'you know *now.*'

Turning his back on his companion, he leaned against the window frame and stared moodily out into the deserted street. Yet again that last argument between him and Mary played itself back through his mind, still so vivid that it might have taken place that same morning instead of all those years before.

'Damn you, woman! What more can I do?'

'You can settle down, Arch! You can give up all your wild ways and–'

'The hell I'll let you tell me how to live my life!'

A laugh. A harsh, derisive, sad little laugh. 'You still don't understand, do you, Arch?'

'What's there to understand?'

'That it's not just about what *you* want any more. You're a married man now, a *father!* If you won't give up the owlhoot for me, at least do it for the boy!'

The boy. He hadn't thought much about the boy since the day she'd run out on him and taken the baby with her. And having convinced himself that he was better off without them, he hadn't even bothered to track them down and bring them back. He wasn't cut out for marriage, anyway. It had been crazy to think that he could fall in love, marry and settle down just like any other man. Hell, he could no sooner give up the owlhoot than he could stop winter following Fall. It wasn't like a job, where you could give notice and then quit. Why couldn't she understand that? What did she expect of him, anyway?

He'd never beaten her before, but that last time ... well, he'd taken just about enough of her whining, and lashed out, and with the first blow struck the rest had followed easily. In that one white-hot moment, love – the love he'd known for her – had turned to hate, because deep down he'd known that she was right: he *did* have responsibilities now. He should at least try to settle down. It wouldn't have been hard. Change your name, grow a beard, put down roots in some distant little place where no one knew Arch Bowman and no one would ever come looking for him.

But the owlhoot was in his blood.

Still, he could at least have tried. He saw

that now. But because of his own stubborn, foolish pride, he'd lost both Mary and the boy. She'd lit out that same night, just taken his horse and disappeared, and that had been that. *Go on, then,* he remembered yelling at the empty stable, *and good riddance!* Even several weeks later, when one of his cronies said he'd heard tell of a red-headed woman and her baby turning up more dead than alive in a town called Freedom Rock, Nebraska, he hadn't bothered to go after them. Let her go! Let 'em both go! Arch Bowman didn't need either of them.

And he'd gotten along real well ... until Colfax, Colorado.

Coming so close to dying like he had, had started him thinking about the boy again. If he was still alive, if it was possible, he was going to take the boy back, raise him just the way he should've raised him all along, and when his luck finally ran out, as he knew that one day it must, the boy would be his monument, someone to mourn his passing, lay flowers on his grave and remind the world that a man called Arch Bowman had once lived and looted right the way across these United States.

It was, he told himself, a grand notion. And, though the newspaperman had told him that Mary was long dead, he'd also confirmed that the boy was still alive and still living in these parts, part of some farmer's family.

Which meant that the boy was his for the taking.

'Your son or not,' opined Ace Hotchkiss, 'you're playin' a dangerous game, Arch. We rob a bank or a stagecoach, folks stand for that; we take a kid against his will, we'll have every man who can pull a trigger agin us.'

Charlie Breen drew on a half-smoked cigarette and nodded. 'Me, I go along with Ace. 'Sides which, the kinda life we live don't allow fer no younkers.'

'I'm not takin' him so's he can ride with us,' growled Bowman, turning back to face them. 'I'm takin' him so's I can set him up someplace, go see him whenever the fancy takes me.'

'You think his folks g-gonna let him go, j-jus' like that?' asked Craven, scratching nervously at his brittle beard. 'They' gonna s-scream so loud, it'll be j-jus' like Ace says – every man can fire a g-gun's gonna be out on our trail.'

'Quit, then,' Bowman invited contemptuously. ''Cause I'm doin it with or without you. My mind's set on it.'

'An' to hell with the boy's folks?' murmured Treber.

'Uh-huh.'

Bowman looked at each man in turn, then said, 'Now, you're either with me, or you ain't. An' if you ain't, I guess it's time we split the blanket.' He picked up his hat and strode slowly to the door. 'You jus' think on it a while, an' when you decide what it is you're gonna do, you come down to the saloon an' tell me.'

He closed the door softly behind him, heard them begin to discuss his proposition as soon as his hand left the doorknob. He knew that Ace Hotchkiss was right: folks wouldn't stand for the abduction of a child, and that was exactly what he was suggesting. The boy wouldn't come along of his own free will. Why should he? He didn't know Bowman from Adam. But he would, eventually. Bowman would see to it.

He went downstairs and crossed the lobby, knowing he was pushing Ned and the others into doing something they had no stomach for, and from which there was no money to be made. If they decided against helping him, as it appeared that they might be, he'd have to go it alone. But he'd survive that, and in time he'd surround himself with a new band of followers.

It was just then, as he stepped out into the street, bathed red by a setting sun that threw shadows long toward the east, that he noticed a good-looking woman and three children vanishing into the general store.

Suddenly shaken, he hauled up sharp.

It was too much to hope that he'd run smack into the boy – his boy. But that boy's colouring, the red of his hair ... it stirred a sudden, almost painful, memory in him. Lord, he'd forgotten just how beautiful Mary had been, her hair just that exact shade...

Swallowing hard, he thought again. *Yeah, it's too much to hope for.* But stranger things had happened. He told himself, *Christ, I should know,* and reached up to touch the healing bullet wound just beneath his ribcage.

Almost before he knew it, he was moving again, taking long, urgent strides along the empty boardwalk, past the saloon and on toward the general store, determined to get a closer look at the kid, to see if there was anything about him that he might recognize.

And then he was there.

For one brief moment he filled the doorframe, hesitated, then pushed inside, his bootfalls setting up a deep, heavy tattoo against the worn boards underfoot. The store, he noted, was cluttered with a million-and-one things, all arranged on wall-mounted shelves and behind glass cases on the counter. A tin stove occupied the centre of the floor, beyond which the woman was buying candy for the red-headed kid. The other two – a lanky-looking youth and a pouty kind of girl – were wandering around, inspecting the storekeeper's wares.

All heads turned when he came inside. 'Uh … help you, mister?' asked the storekeeper, who had a pasty, tired-looking face, powdery grey hair and dark, scared eyes.

Bowman spared him a fleeting glance. 'I'll wait my turn.'

Then, bellying up to the counter, he allowed his gaze to fall on the red-headed kid. He looked down at the boy's face and saw Mary in him, Mary and just *maybe* something of himself, though he dismissed that last notion almost immediately, knowing he was only seeing what he wanted to see.

Even so, the resemblance was there, in the violet-blue eyes, the tip-tilted nose, the shape of the jaw–

It was undeniable.

*This was his son.*

Swallowing hard, his breathing shallow and excited, he said conversationally, 'Looks like the boy's got a sweet tooth, ma'am.'

Ellie looked up at him and glanced away again almost immediately. Like the store-keeper, she had a scared look to her, but that was fine – Bowman was used to it. 'Yes,' she replied, 'he has.' Then, abruptly, 'Come along, children.'

'What's your hurry?' asked Bowman, dropping to a crouch so that he could address Sam on his own level. 'You live hereabouts, Red?'

Red. It's what he'd always called Mary.

Sam shook his head. 'No, sir.'

'Live out of town?'

'Uh-huh.'

'You got a name, boy?'

Sam nodded. 'Sam Canaday.'

'Well, Sam Canaday,' Bowman said affably, offering the boy his hand, 'my name's Bowman, an' I'm real pleased to meet you.'

Shyly, Sam took the big hand and they shook. His touch electrified Bowman. Then the tall man reached into the pocket of his voluminous grey duster and he brought out a silver dollar. 'Here,' he said, 'you buy

119

yourself somethin' nice on me.'

Sam hesitated, glanced questioningly at Matt and Joey, who had come closer during the exchange, then finally at Ellie, who said stiffly, 'I'm sorry, but he has been raised not to accept gifts from strangers.'

'I'm not a stranger,' said Bowman, straightening back to his full height. 'Am I, Red?'

Just then the doorway darkened, and everyone glanced in its direction as Walt came inside, his face appearing somehow tight, his eyes a little wild. All at once the store was filled with a heavy, cloying, expectant silence as he and Bowman traded stares, Walt's mind still whirling with everything Bill Summerfield had just told him: about Bowman's visit to the *Dispatch*, the way the man had beaten Drake to within an inch of his life, the revelations Drake had made upon regaining consciousness from Bowman's final, sadistic pummelling.

At last he found his voice. 'I'll thank you to keep your money,' he said hoarsely. 'The boy's not for sale.'

Something twitched in Bowman's cheek, and he gave Walt a closer scrutiny. Finally he placed Walt as the man who'd cut up rough outside the saloon the previous evening, the marshal's friend. 'Never said he was,' he rasped.

'You didn't have to,' said Walt, licking his lips nervously. 'I know why you're here, Bowman.'

'Is that a fact?'

'Uh-huh. An' I'm tellin' you now, you … you just give it up an' move on.'

Bowman's dark eyes narrowed. 'You *threatenin'* me, farmer?' he asked with a smirk.

By now Walt's jaw muscles were clenching and relaxing at a furious rate. 'I'm *tellin'* you,' he repeated softly, hating the nervousness he heard in his voice, the breathlessness and lack of conviction behind the warning. 'You try messin' with my family an' … an' I'll *kill* you.'

Bowman left the silver dollar on the counter and came forward slowly, confidently, the thin mouth beneath his big black moustache working into a snarl. 'You got no call to take that tone with me, farmer,' he growled. 'I don't give a cuss for your family, but I'm not leavin' this town without my boy.'

He threw himself forward then, collided with Walt and sent the pair of them backwards, through the door and out into the street. Startled, Joey gave a high sort of yelp and, white-faced. Ellie quickly drew her close in a hug the girl made no move to break.

Outside, Walt and Bowman hit the boardwalk in a tangle, rolled and dropped into the dirt with Bowman on top. Ignoring the pain in his side and his still-healing left hand, he started punching Walt for all he was worth, determined to finish it fast, grab the boy and then get the hell out of the territory. He got in a couple of good blows, too, before Walt, bucking and thrusting beneath him, finally threw him sideways and off.

A mad scramble followed, each man trying to be the first one back on his feet. They both made it together, Bowman closing in again fast, punching left-right, left-right, giving Walt no option but to block and retreat, block and retreat—

Then Walt caught Bowman a glancing blow to the ribs and, as he hunched up, Bowman's face screwed into a mask of pain. Walt didn't know he'd just hit Bowman where the late George Hobart's .31-calibre slug had come to rest. But he sensed that he'd uncovered a weakness in his opponent and went right after him, determined to exploit it.

Dust rose up in a violent saffron pall as they clashed again, Walt hitting Bowman with a flurry of punches now, and Bowman feeling every damn' one of them. Drawn by the confrontation, pale faces began to appear at doors and windows as Bowman hooked a right into Walt's belly and Walt buckled forward.

Bowman made to bring his left knee up into Walt's face, but Walt saw it coming, brought his crossed arms up and took most of the force of it on his forearms. He straightened back up, there was a single, fleeting second when each man glared at the other, and then they were trading punches again, each of them bleeding from mouth and nose, Bowman from one ear, Walt from a cut above his right eye.

They pushed apart, danced, weaved, ducked and thrust. Then Bowman caught Walt another wicked right that sank wrist-deep into his flat stomach and literally slammed the air out of him. He folded with a painful, groaning gasp of sound, his face went deep red, and when Bowman's knee came up this time it hit him right in the face. Walt staggered backwards, completely disorientated now, twisted, fell to his knees and collapsed over the public trough.

The shock of sinking head-and-shoulders deep into tepid water brought him back to sudden, choking awareness, and he turned on his knees just as Bowman came in close with one boot raised to stomp him.

He scooped a handful of scummy water up into Bowman's hate-contorted face and, as Bowman tried to dodge it, and lost his balance, Walt thrust back to his wobbly legs and went to meet him with fists folded. He hit Bowman a roundhouse right, felt the man's head snap sideways, felt the force of the blow jar all the way up to his shoulder, then hit him with his left, then another right. Bowman started jelly-legging all over the place, trying to put up some sort of defence, but his arms were loose and waving and Walt knew he was finished; that against all the odds, he'd actually beaten his opponent.

Then a gunblast cut through the rush of blood in his ears, and a miniature explosion of dirt erupted at his feet. He took a wide, drunken pace backward, then froze.

Gasping, he turned a swollen, bloodied face to the boardwalk where Bowman's four accomplices had lined up to watch him. Smoke was drifting sluggishly from the long barrel of the black man's Colt .45.

His water-dark shoulders dropped, because he knew he couldn't take them all on. As much as anything else, he wasn't armed, wasn't much of a hand with firearms, anyway. No. They had him – and if they had *him,* it meant they also had Sam.

He looked up and down the street, having to tilt his head back a little to allow for his swelling-shut eyes, but he knew he wouldn't get any help from the people of Freedom Rock, not now. He'd made his point all too well that very morning, when he'd told them not to get involved because they had wives and children to consider.

A few yards away, Bowman spat a cussword at him, squared his shoulders and started to reach for his Frontier .44. Breathing noisily through his nose, Walt looked at him, saw by the blood and bruises on Bowman's face that he had acquitted himself well, but not well enough.

'Say ... goodbye, sodbuster!' wheezed Bowman.

'No!'

All eyes turned to the store-front and Walt, still dripping water and blood, half-whispered, 'M-Matt...'

He had no idea where Matt had gotten

hold of the Winchester he was now holding waist-high. He knew that Tom Hardin sold guns and figured the boy must have helped himself to one from Tom's stock when it became obvious that no one else was going to act in his defence. Now, as Ellie appeared at the boy's shoulder, Matt fairly glared at Bowman, still knowing nothing of the man's cold-blooded murder of Pat Patterson, nothing of his interest in Sam, knowing only that Bowman meant his father harm, and knowing also that never in a thousand years would he allow that.

'You touch that gun an' I'll shoot you down!' the boy said, nervously but with determination. 'I *mean* it!'

Bowman's sneer tore the splits in his punished lips a little wider. 'Best you get on inside with the womenfolk,' he rasped. ''Cause iffen you stay where you are, I'll wax you an' your old man both.'

Matt's reaction was swift and to the point. He fired the rifle and, more by luck than design, sprayed dirt all over Bowman's boot-tips. 'You just get!' Matt grated through set teeth and, as he fumble-worked the rifle's lever to put another shell in the breech, Walt saw tears standing bright in his sharp green eyes, but tears of fury, not fear.

'*You heard him!*' called Bill Summerfield, as he shuffled along the street carrying an old Henry repeater in his gnarled hands. 'Alla you fellers, you just get, an' thank your stars that we don't arrest you for murder!'

A quick, dangerous ripple seemed to wash through the four gunnies standing on the boardwalk, and Walt had a terrible, sinking feeling that this thing was going to come to shooting, and when it did, a lot of good folks were going to die.

But then Tom Hardin pushed out of his store, rifle in hand, and from across the street came Len Parsons and Vern Crombie, each man holding a pistol, and Bernie Wilkes, hefting a long-barrelled shotgun.

'We've stood just about all we plan to stand from you, Bowman,' said Bill Summerfield in a surprisingly steady voice. 'But no more. Now, you do like the boy here says, an' you *get.*'

For a moment longer, Bowman stood there in the middle of the street, his right hand halfway to his Colt. But as they glanced around them, he and his men saw other faces watching them, other hands clutching other weapons, and slowly, slowly the desire to raze this town to the ground settled to something altogether colder and altogether darker.

Still breathing hard from the fight, Bowman nodded and said, 'Aw right. We're goin'.'

'You do that,' called Bernie Wilkes, grimly. 'An' you just keep ridin', mister, 'cause if you show your ugly face in this town again, you're just likely to get it shot off!'

# SIX

When she heard a soft rapping at her hotel-room door, Ellie – still feeling jumpy and upset – gave a nervous twitch, and her right hand flew to her mouth. A moment later, having composed herself once more, she rose from the chair beside the dresser and crossed to the door, where, she cleared her throat and asked nervously, 'Wh-who's there?'

'It's me, Ellie,' came a muffled reply. 'Walt.'

She turned the key in the lock and swung the door open to reveal him standing in the hallway beyond, his hat in one hand, a package in the other, and a sheepish expression on his battered but cleaned-up face.

They looked at each other for a long, silent moment, and then he said, carefully, 'I, ah, jus' stopped by to make sure you was all right. Before me an' the kids head on back to the farm, I mean.'

It was a little past 8.30, barely an hour

since Walt's fight with Bowman and the subsequent showdown which had forced the outlaws to quit town in a surly, backward-scowling bunch. Walt had watched them go, still shocked by what had happened, and then he'd allowed Bill Summerfield to lead him down to the livery stable, patch the worst of his injuries and rub a little salve on the rest.

While that was going on, some of the pluckier townswomen, having heard, or guessed, what this was all about, had come out to surround, comfort and generally coddle Walt's three children. Feeling somewhat excluded from that, Ellie had eventually made her way back to the hotel, now more uncertain than ever about the life she was letting herself in for. In fact, she had been thinking hard about that very prospect ever since, and had just reached a sombre but inevitable conclusion.

Now she said, 'You'd, ah, better come in.'

He limped past her, moving carefully to favour his sore body, and stood awkwardly in the centre of the room. In the harsh lamplight, the ridge of inflamed brow that overhung his bruised and bloodshot eyes threw a dismal shadow down over his long face, and the top lip of his sad-looking mouth, being swollen, made him speak with a lisp.

'What can I say?' he asked, with a helpless shake of the head.

'Perhaps you could tell me what that, uh, altercation, was all about?' she suggested.

He wasn't completely sure what the word *altercation* meant, but he guessed it had something to do with the fight. 'That man, Bowman,' he said in a low, tired voice. 'Turns out he's Sam's pa–'

'*What?*'

'Ayuh. An' he came back to claim him.'

Studying his injuries a little closer, she noted shakily, 'He came back, all right. With a vengeance.'

'Well, it's over an' done with now. There won't be no more scenes like the one you witnessed this afternoon, Ellie.'

'No,' she said. 'There won't be.'

He read something firm and regretful in her tone and nodded defeatedly. 'I kinda guessed you'd say somethin' like that.'

'I'm sorry, Walt, but–'

'No, no, you got nothin' to be sorry for. You didn't plan on lettin' yourself in for any o' this. None of us did. This whole thing, what happened last night, what happened this evenin', it … well, it wasn't the best way to start a courtship, was it?'

She turned away from him and went over to the window, where she fidgeted with a little lace handkerchief. 'H-how are the children?'

He shrugged. 'Spooked. They don't really understand what the fight was all about, 'cept for Matt. But they'll get over it, in time.'

'Of course,' she agreed, turning back to him. 'You will … remember me to them, won't you?'

'Sure.' He handed her the package then, and said softly, 'This is for you.'

'What? Oh, Walt, I don't—'

'It's not much,' he said, 'but I want you to have it.' He walked slowly back to the door, where he swung around and faced her again. 'Should be a stage through here tomorrow afternoon, take you north an' west to the railhead. I wish you a good journey, Ellie, an' a good future.'

'Walt—' she began.

'Yes'm?'

She hesitated. 'Will you be all right? The children?'

'We'll be fine. That Bowman, he took it into his head to come lookin' for his boy, but he was about nine years too late. Reckon he knows that, now.'

'But what if he *doesn't?* What if he comes back?'

He shrugged. 'I'll cross that bridge when I have to.' Abruptly he stuck out his right hand. 'I'm real sorry it didn't pan out, Ellie,' he said with feeling, and when she put her hand to his, he squeezed her fingers briefly and then let himself out of the room ... and out of her life.

She stood a while just staring at the closed door, and then she realized she was still holding the package he'd given her. With a frown she took it across to the bed, set it down, carefully untied the string and unfolded the brown paper wrapping. Inside she found two cakes of pressed, perfumed soap, a small box of herbal nostrum, a shawl, a reticule, a novel, some magazines, a rose-shaped looking glass–

She dropped heavily to the edge of the mattress and bent her head, suddenly struck by thoughts of what might have been. A moment later she gave vent to a single, loud sob and then buried her face in her hands, thinking wretchedly, *Walt ... oh, Walt.*

But it was too late to change her mind now. She had made her decision, and he was gone. Besides which, he had other, more pressing, matters to concern him right now, without a silly, changeable woman to complicate things.

She retired to bed shortly after that, changed into her nightdress, folded and packed away her skirt and blouse and set out her green and black travelling outfit, all ready for the following day.

Finally, extinguishing the lamp, she drew back the thin drapes and stared out at the night-darkened street below. Light showed at several windows, and she heard the tinny jangle of a piano mingling with the animated babble of men's voices coming from the Freedom Saloon. One way or another, it had been quite a day in Freedom Rock and the townsfolk were still too excited about their victory over the Bowman gang to think much about sleep.

With a dazed shake of the head, she turned and climbed into the lumpy hotel bed. This town, this land, these people, Walt, his children – everything was so different to what she had been used to. So different, in fact, that she had given way to a moment of panic and decided she would be better off back in her native Minnesota, where life was safe and predictable.

As she lay waiting for sleep, however, she couldn't help but think of all the things she would be giving up by going home. How did she really feel about Walt? He was a good, kind, gentle man. In time, she felt sure she could love him. His children, too – Sam, with his infectious enthusiasm, Matt, with his unswerving devotion to his father...

Only Joey had shown her any hostility. But given time, she was sure she could have won the girl over.

Now, though ... now she would never know for sure.

Out in the darkness just beyond the town limits, Bowman watched Freedom Rock through eyes that glittered dangerously. Behind him, Ned Treber and the rest of the boys sat their saddles in restless anticipation, eager for the chance to get even.

No one treated them the way the people of Freedom Rock had treated them earlier that evening. No one ever told Arch Bowman or Ned Treber to get out of town. If they knew what was good for them, folks walked real soft around them, or paid the price.

Now, as odd little sounds strayed to him on the chilly wind, Arch Bowman's piercing brown eyes narrowed: a piano, the occasional laugh, an isolated comment that carried further than the rest...

His lips thinned.

The sonsofbitches were reliving their moment of glory, reminding each other about how they'd stood up to the Bowman boys.

It was, he knew, a story they'd tell again and again, and that with each telling it would grow bigger and bolder and more impressive. And he knew also that he could not allow these people to get away with running him and his men out of town, any more than he could allow word of their humiliation here to spread. In this business, a man had to be hard to survive. He had to carve himself a reputation and build on it, not let a lousy bunch of townies push him around whenever the fancy took them.

Then, of course, there was the boy to consider. *Red.*

Bowman hadn't really known how he'd feel when he finally tracked the kid down, but nothing could have prepared him for the almost giddying rush of feeling he'd experienced when he first saw him. Red's colouring had started it, had brought back such a vivid image of Mary that all at once he felt her loss desperately. It hadn't been

136

that way this morning, when the news-paperman had told him she was dead. Then he'd felt nothing at all. He wasn't interested in Mary. But seeing the boy this evening, and seeing Mary in him—

Ah, but the sight of the kid himself, his son, that had been a comfort. And now, as he sat his horse, he felt a surge of pride in the boy: in his fine build and the good, direct look of him.

But enough of that. Sensing the restless-ness of the men behind him, he came back to the business at hand. The boy had waited this long: he could wait just a while longer. For now, there was Freedom Rock to deal with.

Turning his head, he said, 'You ready for this?'

He sensed rather than saw the nodding of their heads, the movement of Treber's gunhand closing around the butt of his .45, and his thin smile was lost in the darkness. A few hours earlier, he'd been in danger of losing these men. But now, having shared the shame of being thrown out of town, and the fierce, all-consuming need to get back at the people who'd seen them off at gunpoint, they were united again, and this time, Bow-man knew, they would side him all the way, up to and including the taking of the boy.

'Charlie,' he called flatly. 'Light 'em up.'

There came the scratch of a match, a small, winking flame ... and then the crude torches Ed Craven and Ace Hotchkiss held in their free hands flared to life with a low, rumbling crackle.

His face bathed orange by the flickering glow, Bowman slowly drew his .44. In the fitful light of the burning torches, he looked from one man to the next, and then showed his teeth in a snarl. 'Say so long to Freedom Rock boys,' he rasped. 'An' say hello to *Payback*.'

Barely three minutes later they drew rein outside the Freedom Saloon, their horses bumping and sidestepping briefly before spreading out in a loose line. Then, at a sign from Bowman, Ace Hotchkiss hurled his flaming torch through the batwing doors and into the centre of the crowded room.

For the space of maybe four heartbeats, nothing happened.

On the fifth heartbeat there was a shout of alarm, the piano-playing stopped and all at once the easy babble of conversation grew loud and panicky. Outside, listening to the clatter of hasty footfalls and the scrape and shudder of chair- and table-legs, Bowman grinned wickedly.

Then the night exploded with flame and thunder as he, Treber, Breen and Hotchkiss peppered the front of the building with gunfire.

Inside the saloon, wood splintered and pocked, and shards of shattered glass spun through the air like knife-sharp particles of ice. The zip and whine of flying lead was all but drowned by the startled yells of men running for cover.

Still seated at the piano, Joe Banks twitched and then stiffened, the sudden jolt of his emaciated little body helping to flick his bullet-blasted brains right across the yellowed keys. As he fell sideways to the floor, his body still frozen stiff with shock, the back-bar mirrors caved in on themselves and nearby bottles and glasses exploded. Another townsman collapsed, grabbing at the fleshy part of his left leg with a howling kind of scream. One more fell, crunching broken glass beneath him, and then a fourth.

In the space of maybe thirty seconds, the saloon had become a place of noise, confusion, fear and death.

In the centre of the floor, the torch

continued to burn almost lazily, igniting the sawdust around it and blackening the boards beneath. Bullet-struck lanterns burst apart, spraying fiery gobbets of kerosene everywhere, and smoke began to rise in dark, billowing clouds.

Seeing the flames spreading in the centre of the room, Les Parsons left the cover of the bar and made a desperate attempt to stamp them out. Behind him, someone yelled, *'Les! Fer God's sake, get down!'* but he paid them no mind, and in the very next moment another wild slug found its mark, hitting him in the chest, puncturing his right lung and flinging him to the floor, where he started shaking and coughing blood.

Reloading outside, Bowman bawled, *'Come on!'* and almost as one, they wheeled their horses and powered on up the street until they reached Bill Summerfield's livery stable.

The noise had already brought Bill running from his quarters at the back of the big barn, and he was just stumbling out into the street when Bowman and the rest hauled rein again. Seeing them come, suddenly finding himself ringed by horsemen, Bill came to a clumsy, skidding halt. Bowman glared down at him for a moment, deliberately allowing Bill one brief second of gut-clenching terror; then, as Bill turned and tried to run back into the stable, Bowman squeezed trigger and shot him through the spine.

Bill hit the hay-strewn floor between the stalls, slid forward on his chin and then started writhing weakly. Ed Craven hurled his torch through the big double doorway, then started scratching furiously at his beard. The burning brand landed with a bounce, cartwheeled a few times and came to rest in a pile of hay.

The single flame started spreading almost immediately, illuminating the interior of the big barn and hurling fitful shadows up over the walls. Stalled horses, already made nervous by the single gunshot and the harsh, metallic stink of spilled blood that followed it, started stamping and kicking in a frenzy of fear.

Calm as you like, Bowman emptied his weapon into them and, giggling, Charlie Breen did likewise.

As shot horses reared up and then crashed down, the unmistakable boom of a shotgun suddenly punched through the higher crack of pistol-fire and Treber turned his mount hurriedly to face the new threat. On the other side of the street, up on the boardwalk outside the combination Western Union and US Post Office, he spotted a big man in shirtsleeves, with a bald head and a dark thick beard, raising a Loomis No 15 shotgun at him.

They hadn't been in town long enough for him to get to know Bernie Wilkes by name, but Treber remembered him from earlier that evening. Bernie was the man who'd threatened to blow Arch's face off if he ever showed it around town again.

He thrust his gun-arm forward, thumbed back the Colt's hammer and pulled the trigger.

The weapon in his fist clicked softly.

*Empty.*

With a curse, he stuffed the gun away, reached across his body, unsheathed the cavalry sabre and dug his heels into the prancing horse beneath him.

*'Yaaahhh!'*

Bernie saw him coming at a flat-out gallop, the sabre held high above his head, and fired the shotgun again. Flame spat from the weapon's long barrel and the stock kicked back into his shoulder with all the force of an angry fist, but he knew instinctively that he'd fired too soon and that the shot had gone wide.

He thought despairingly, Oh, Jesus God—Ned Treber was still coming.

For one fleeting moment, Bernie considered his chances of breaking the shotgun open, tearing out the empty cases and stuffing in reloads, but he knew he'd never make it before Treber reached him.

The sensible thing, then, was to turn and run, while he still had a chance.

But seeing coughing, smouldering men staggering out of the saloon, seeing greedy flames snaking all over Bill Summerfield's livery stable and, like as not, over Bill himself too, God rest him, Bernie up-ended the shotgun and, ignoring the heat of the barrels so that he could hold it like a club, elected to fight.

Not stopping to think about it, he leapt down off the boardwalk and ran to meet Treber, his big belly bouncing up and down, his mouth yanked wide in a scream of defiance, the heavy shotgun held high. Up in his Visalia saddle, Treber knew a brief moment of surprise, because that was the last thing he'd been expecting.

A handful of seconds later, man and horse collided, and the man came off worst. The force of the impact threw Bernie backwards and shocked all the rage out of him.

Suddenly he realized just how impossible his position really was.

As Treber loomed over him and Bowman and the others watched on, Bernie looked up into the ebony face of the man who was just about to kill him and tears sprang bright to his eyes. A moment later, the sabre came down in a flashing silver blur, and the razor-sharp blade sliced a deep, diagonal gash across the clerk-telegrapher's torso.

Blood erupted from the wound, but Bernie only grunted softly, his shoulders rose an inch or so, his head sank a little lower and the empty shotgun fell from his nerveless grasp. Treber's horse, splashed by the blood, minced around in a tight, protesting circle, and then, leaning forward and sideways, Treber made another, more forceful thrust with the sabre, this time running Bernie right the way through to the spine and beyond.

For a while Bernie just stood there, his face all twisted up as blood trickled from between his taut lips to soak into his beard. Then, slowly, he fell backwards, off the blade that had skewered him, and collapsed in a red, leaking heap.

Treber studied him dispassionately for a

few seconds, then turned the horse around and trotted it back to Arch and the others, sheathing the sabre as he went.

By the light of the burning stable, they surveyed the town. A few locals were trying to fight the blaze that was consuming the saloon; a few more were sitting on the opposite boardwalk, holding their heads in their hands and coughing. Behind them, Pastor Fleming was walking backwards and forwards in front of the church, wringing his hands helplessly. He, too, was weeping.

Without a word, the five outlaws reloaded their guns. And then, when Bowman jabbed his heels into his big horse's flanks and yelled something primitive and unintelligible at the top of his voice, they surged back along Main, shooting out windows and scattering bewildered townsfolk as they went.

Walt sat in the darkness of the combination parlour and kitchen, his old Springfield carbine resting heavily across his knees. Around him, the farm lay silent but for the occasional snort or snuffle of the hogs in their pen, and the odd, laddering turn of the windmill out front.

Sitting stiffly on the spindle-backed settle,

he stifled a yawn. Tonight of all nights he had to keep alert, because he knew that, just like Ellie had said, Bowman would be back.

They'd made the long journey home in a numb sort of hush, Joey and Sam still unnerved by the fight they'd been forced to witness. Only Matt seemed to have grasped what it had all been about, but sensing his father's reluctance to discuss the matter, he had refrained from comment.

Back home again, Walt had tried to involve Joey and Sam in preparing a light supper, but their hearts hadn't been in it. They were scared, the pair of them, and not without good reason. They'd already lost their mother: now they were scared of losing their father, too.

With the meal over, Walt had told them to go wash up and get ready for bed, but they hadn't wanted to go. 'That man's waiting for us,' Joey had protested whiningly; casting a wary glance at the darkened bedroom she shared with Sam.

Walt, knowing she meant Bowman, replied as confidently as he could, 'That man's gone.'

'Miss Bryant's gone too, isn't she, Pa?' said Matt, quietly.

Walt looked at him, looked away again,

and said briefly, 'Uh-huh.'

He took a lamp into the bedroom and held it high while Joey and Sam inspected every impossible place where they thought Bowman might be hiding. When they finally convinced themselves that he was nowhere to be found – especially underneath the bed – they reluctantly yielded to sleep. Matt lingered a while in the parlour, in case his father wanted to talk, but it seemed that Walt had other things on his mind right then, and eventually the boy went to his own room with a soft, ''Night, Pa.'

Now, Walt looked over at Kate's rocker and found himself thinking not about his late wife, but about Ellie. She had become such a large part of his life over the last several months that he could hardly believe that their long postal courtship had ended the way it had. And though he wasn't fool enough to think he loved her – leastways, not yet – the thought of never seeing her again, or receiving her letters, or knowing what became of her once she caught the stage out of Freedom Rock, stabbed at him like a rusty blade.

It was only when his chin touched his chest that he realized he must've fallen asleep. He sat a little straighter, drew air in through his nostrils and let it out in a gusty sigh. He couldn't sleep, not tonight. Tonight he had to stay alert, to protect his kids.

It sounded good in principle. But the simple truth was that he'd just lived through two of the lousiest days of his life. He'd lost his closest friend and the woman he'd been fixing to marry: he'd been involved in a fight that had left him feeling sick and sore; and he knew that sooner or later, Bowman would make another try at reclaiming his boy.

His mouth firmed up at the thought. The hell with 'your' boy, he told himself with cold, uncharacteristic anger. You might've sired him, but he's my son, and if you think I'll let you take him without a fight, you'd better think again.

He dry-washed his face, tightened his grip on the Springfield and told himself to stay awake. But the weariness in him, like the after-effects of the fight, ran bone-deep and could not be ignored.

Gradually … gradually … he dozed off again.

He slept a deep, dreamless sleep for about thirty minutes and then snapped awake with a start. Around him, the darkened house hissed with silence. He cleared his throat and sniffed a bit, not sure what had wakened him until he heard it again – the distant *pockata-pockata* of approaching horses, carrying on the cool night wind.

The sound galvanized him. He leapt up and crossed the parlour fast until he came to the small window just left of the door. Looking beyond the window, so close to it that his quick, nervous breathing misted the glass, he was just in time to see the silhouettes of four horsemen crest a gentle rise to the south-west – the direction of town – then drop down into the darkness this side of the ridge.

Beneath his bruises he went pale. So, he thought, They're coming. But *four* of them? Four, when there should have been *five?*

Fighting his panic, he wondered if the approaching riders had deliberately allowed themselves to be seen and heard to keep him at the front of the house while the fifth man snuck up and came in through the back. He knew nothing about the way men like Bowman worked, but that sounded like as good a strategy as any.

Well, the fifth man was going to find a surprise waiting for him.

He turned away from the window and started back across the room, twisting up

149

his courage, knowing that he would do anything to protect his younkers, up to and including murder. But he only went about seven or eight feet when he caught another sound – the soft nickering of another horse somewhere much closer.

Already out in the front yard.

Dry-mouthed, he started back through the room – and that was when the fifth man kicked in the front door.

The door flew back and slammed against the wall, and a moon-silvered, duster-clad shape filled the frame. Walt made a strangled little sound in his throat and started to raise the carbine, but before he could use the weapon, the man-shape spotted the movement and spat flame at him from waist-height, once, twice, the flat, spiteful snap of the shots shaking the house.

Walt went stumbling backwards, then all the way over, crashed against the settle and lay still. And the very last sound he heard before everything went black was his children, screaming for their daddy.

## SEVEN

For a long, incalculable time, it seemed to Walt that he was trapped at the bottom of the deepest, darkest, quietest mine-shaft in the whole wide world, seeing nothing, hearing nothing, feeling nothing. Then, slowly, a vague sense of consciousness began to return, and suddenly he felt as if he were rising toward a lighter kind of darkness, moving faster, faster, sickeningly fast, rising ever higher until at length the blackness started turning greyer, paler, brighter–

He came up out of it abruptly, not sure who he was, where he was, what he was, and he was completely unprepared for the hard, throbbing ache that pounded without mercy at the back of his head. He rolled over and puked while he was still only half-conscious, and the puking helped a bit, but not much.

Then he opened his eyes, and the first thing he saw was weak dawnlight filling the window beside the door. He stared at the window for a long time, waiting for his

151

sluggish brain to start working properly. He felt sick and confused. Why had he been stretched out on the parlour floor? What had he done to himself? Where had the entire night gone to?

He reached around to the back of his head, winced and brought his questing fingers away smeared with blood. *Blood?* Stupidly he turned and stared at the edge of the settle, a dim, indistinct memory stirring inside him. He'd slipped. That was it. He'd slipped, caught his head and knocked himself unconscious.

It all came back to him then, and he dredged up a soft, despairing moan from someplace deep inside him. Muttering now, he turned onto all fours, shoved up onto his feet and swayed a moment, remembering the man in the doorway and the two shots he'd fired: that he himself had tried to dodge the shots and, apparently, succeeded, but that, in the process, he'd slipped and knocked himself stupid, just when his children needed him.

His children?

His voice a scratchy rasp, he called, '*Sam!*' And then, '*Matt! Joey?*'

But for the rooting hogs out back, the distant clucking of the hens, the slow, laddery

152

turn of the windmill, the house was silent.

Ignoring the sickly churning in his belly, he staggered over to Joey and Sam's bedroom. The door was open and Joey, her face absolutely bloodless, was stretched out on the rumpled sheets, her head on the pillow, her eyes closed, to all intents and purposes, sleeping.

He said fearfully, 'J-Joey...?' And then, louder, *'Joey?'*

He saw the dark, powdery smudge of a bruise along her left jawline then, and went a little crazy. He half-fell across the room, dropped to his knees beside the bed and grabbed the child with rough desperation.

*'Joey! Joey!'*

Still she didn't stir, and he thought, but didn't want to think, that she was dead. He thought, No, no, please... And almost immediately he spotted the shallow rise and fall of her breathing and realized that she was unconscious: sometime after Bowman had shot at him and taken him for dead, the sonofabitch had knocked her senseless. *A twelve-year-old girl.*

Shaking now, beside himself with fury, he shoved himself up and looked around. 'Matt?' No reply. *'Sam?'*

He stumbled back into the parlour, across

to the door. He pulled it open and staggered out into the sharp new day, dreading what he might find.

He looked around. The yard was deserted. He made a shambling, drunken circuit of the house, found no one. He checked the out-buildings. Nothing.

By the end of it he stood in the middle of the yard and tried to marshal his disordered thoughts. He understood why there was no sign of Sam. Bowman had taken him. But where was Matt?

Again he found himself praying. Please God, let them be safe. Let them both be safe… Then he thought about Joey again. How badly had Bowman injured her? He had to get her to town and then he had to get after Bowman, wherever the devil had gone.

He stumbled around to the back of the house and pumped some ice-cold water over his head. The shock of it chased off the worst of the throbbing and cleaned and numbed the cut in the back of his skull. Still trembling, but thinking a little straighter now, he went back inside and made a closer examination of the girl. That started him sobbing again, but once he'd satisfied himself that she was unconscious and no worse, he left her once more and went to hitch up the wagon.

To his bafflement, he found that one of the team-horses had gone missing. But right then there was no time to ponder what had become of it. Still, the remaining horse wouldn't be able to haul the wagon by itself, so he quickly rigged it out for riding instead, then went back inside, gathered Joey up in his arms and somehow got them both clumsily mounted, the girl still sleeping her deep, punched-out sleep in his lap.

By now he was so deep in his troubled thoughts that the long ride to town passed in a blur, and it was only when he spotted a faint black pall hanging in the sky a mile or so ahead – roughly where town should be – that his thinking finally sharpened and something dark and unpleasant began to uncoil in the pit of his stomach.

Freedom Rock itself came into sight a quarter-hour later, and when he saw the black smudge where Bill Summerfield's stable used to be, and the charred, skeletal remains of the Freedom Saloon, the smallest, softest, tiredest groan sounded in his throat.

Main Street, he saw, was deserted. Indeed, there was an air of desolation about the entire, shot-up town. But there was plenty of coming and going outside the church, where townsfolk seemed to have congregated and were milling around – in shock, he thought. As he drew level with the unadorned clapboard building, with its pitched roof and modest spire, Tom Hardin came down the steps toward him.

'God Almighty, Walt!' breathed the tired-looking storekeeper. 'What happened?'

Lips working hard, Walt said, 'Bow … Bowman. Sonofabitch hit my place las' night. He … he took my boys, Tom.' He said it like he still couldn't believe it.

'An' Joey, here?' asked Tom, reaching up to take her from him.

Walt shook his head. 'I think Bowman hit her. She … she won't come round.'

'Let's get her inside,' Hardin said urgently, holding her while Walt dismounted. 'We been usin' the church like an infirmary, to deal with the wounded.'

'Wh-what happened here, anyway?' Walt asked, thinking he already knew the answer.

'Same as happened to you,' said Hardin, passing Joey back to him. 'Bowman. Him an' his damn' rawhiders tore through town las' night.'

'Bill?' asked Walt, thinking he knew the

156

answer to that one, too.

Tom said thickly, 'They killed him, Walt. Shot him in the back–'

Walt faltered, broke stride and let go another little sigh of pain. A long moment passed, and then he asked, 'Anyone else?'

'Bernie an' Les,' Hardin reported in a voice that broke slightly. 'Joe Bell an' Harve Norman, too. Bastards killed 'em all, left behind seven wounded, an' burned down the saloon an' livery. We been up half the night, fightin' to keep the fires from spreadin'.'

They got moving again, up the steps and into the church. It was plain, as churches went, just an altar upon which stood a tall plaster cross and a few knocked-together pews where exhausted-looking townsmen were either awaiting or recovering from treatment for gunshots, cuts or burns of varying severity.

Walt carried Joey down the aisle to a vacant pew at the front, where a tall, thick-waisted man with short, centre-parted brown hair and a longhorn moustache was pinching at the skin between his tired eyes. This was George Collins, Freedom Rock's only physician, his shirtsleeves rolled back, his slim hands stained with old blood.

As he set Joey down and the doctor came to take a closer look at her, Walt heard someone off to his left call his name. He turned as Ellie hurried over, setting down a bowl and cloth with which she'd just been helping to clean up a man who'd blistered both hands and most of his face whilst fighting the fires.

She, like everyone there, looked worn out. Her hair was a mess, with strands hanging loose either side of her heart-shaped face, and her intelligent green eyes looked hollow and washed out. Right then, however, his heart lifted at the sight of her, and he had to glance away briefly and blink several times to clear his vision.

'Walt, what happened?' she asked. Collins began to examine Joey's face with his finger-tips, then carefully peel her eyelids back to study the eyes themselves.

Not trusting himself to speak for any length of time, he told it all as quickly as he could, finishing wretchedly, 'I let them down. I wanted to protect them but when … when Bowman burst in, I slipped and fell, and now they're gone–'

Instinctively, Ellie opened her arms to him and, not even thinking about it, he stepped straight into her embrace. She rubbed at his back and patted him as if he were a child himself, and said, 'He won't get away with it, Walt. He *can't*. But why do you suppose he took Matt, too?'

He shook his head. 'I … I don't think he did. I think maybe Matt took one of the horses and went after them by himself.'

'Oh, no…'

Collins made a sound just then, and Walt and Ellie broke apart, each of them sniffing and clearing their throats and looking down at the floor. 'She'll be all right, Walt,' said the doctor, gently. 'A mild concussion is all. We'll put her somewhere nice and warm, and let her sleep it off.'

'I'll take her back to my room at the hotel,' offered Ellie. 'She'll be well looked after, Walt, I promise you.'

Walt swayed a bit. 'Th-thanks.'

'And Walt,' said Collins, 'you heed what your woman here just told you: Bowman won't get away with this. Vern Crombie's already lit out for Julesburg. When the law catches up with that damn' butcher, they'll get your little one back safe.' He stretched to ease his aching back. 'Now, you don't look so hot yourself. Come here and let's take a look at you.'

'I got to go,' said Walt, shaking his head

and shrugging all at once.

'Go?' repeated Ellie. 'Go where?'

Ignoring her question, he just reached out, took one of her hands and said, 'Thanks for everything, Ellie.'

'I haven't done anything.'

'She's done her share and more,' Collins cut in. 'I tell you, Walt, it's a woman and a half you've got here.'

Knowing that was true, Walt bent, planted a gentle kiss on Joey's forehead, then heeled around and hurried back along the aisle, suddenly restless with new resolve.

Outside, Tom Hardin was moodily stuffing his scratched old pipe with rough-cut tobacco. The minute he saw Walt, he said, 'How–?'

'She'll be all right,' he replied. Then, 'Tom, I need some things from the store.'

'Sure. What kind of things?'

'A handgun, a halfway decent rifle, supplies.'

Hardin's tired eyes went big. 'Hey, now! You're not goin' *after* them sonsabitches–'

'Yes, I am.'

'Damn-it, Walt, you're no hand with a gun! You're a *farmer*, for Cris'sakes! You go against a man like Bowman, he'll chew you up an' spit you out, jus' like he did with Bill an' the others, an' then where'll your kids be?'

Not answering that, not even wanting to think about it, Walt said softly, 'All right if I help myself?'

Hardin looked at him for a long moment, saw that he was absolutely set on it, and sighed defeatedly. 'Take whatever you need. You got any idea where Bowman was headed when he left your place?'

'Not a one. I figure to go back there an' see what I can find in the way of tracks.' He ran a hand across his bristly face. 'That reminds me. I'll need a fresh horse.'

'Bowman's men shot most of 'em las' night. The ones they didn't shoot burned to death. But I reckon we can find you somethin' that can run, an' a saddle that won't bust your balls too much. Just do me one favour, Walt: when you catch up with 'em, don't give the bastards any chance at all.'

'I don't plan to.'

Without further discussion, he crossed the street, went into the deserted store and quickly filled a gunnysack with provisions, so caught up in his own concerns by this time that he barely acknowledged the arrival of a hard-pushed horse somewhere outside.

Instead, he turned his attention to Tom's stock of weapons. The selection wasn't particularly large, but for a man who didn't know much about guns in the first place, it was bewildering. Hesitantly, he selected a Marlin Model 1881 lever-action rifle in .45-.70 calibre, and a Colt Peacemaker, which he stuffed into the waistband of his dusty black trousers.

He was just helping himself to boxes of ammunition for his new acquisition when the hasty clatter of footsteps on the plankwalk outside, coupled with Tom Hardin's voice calling urgently, 'Walt! Walt!' made him turn toward the doorway.

A moment later Tom came hustling in, his face positively beaming as he propelled a dishevelled, foot-dragging second figure ahead of him. He said with breathless excitement, 'Look who's jus' turned up, Walt!'

It was Matt.

Hardly daring to believe his eyes, Walt murmured the boy's name, softly at first, then a little louder. Tearful and trying to fight it, Matt said hoarsely, 'Pa, I … I thought you was–' and then Walt threw the Marlin onto the counter and went to grab him.

There was so much he wanted to say in

that moment, but right then speech was impossible, for both of them. All they could do was just hold each other tight, with Matt shivering in his father's arms, the emotion in him too strong to suppress.

After a while, Walt held the boy at arm's length and studied him with a frown. Matt was just about done-in. He looked pale and exhausted, and his bloodshot eyes still held a little craziness. Also, there was a nasty, purplish bump on his right temple. 'What happened, son?' he asked gently.

Matt sleeved roughly at his dirty, tear-streaked face, and sniffed wetly. 'I kn-knew that feller Bowman wouldn't give up without a fight,' he managed at length. 'I knew he'd be back, couldn't sleep for thinkin' of it. Then, w-when he burst in like he did...' He shook his head, said helplessly, 'I thought he'd *killed* you, Pa! Guess I jus' went wild, threw myself at him, got this for my trouble.' He gestured to his bruised temple. 'It w-was awful! Joey kept s-screamin', wouldn't stop, so he hit her too, knocked her cold, then grabbed Sam. S-Sam tried to fight him, but that B-Bowman, he jus' scooped him up under one arm, an' then him an' the men with him, they lit out. I ... I did what I could for Joey an' then I ...

163

I went after 'em.'

'You're a brave boy, Matt,' said Walt, squeezing his shoulder.

'Oh, I wasn't fixin' to fight 'em,' the boy replied earnestly. 'I knew I couldn't take 'em all on. But I thought, if I could find out which way they was headed, I could c-come back here an' maybe they'd raise a posse, go after 'em in force.'

'These folks got troubles of their own right now, son.'

'But we gotta do *somethin'!* They took Sam!'

'They took him, all right. But I figure on gettin' him back.'

Matt frowned. 'All by *yourself?*' Suddenly he got that feverish, agitated look back in his eyes. 'Take me with you, Pa!' he said desperately. 'I can show you where–'

His father's voice was firm. 'No. You've already done enough, boy. You jus' tell me where they was headed, an' I'll do the rest.'

Knowing that arguing about it would only waste valuable time, Matt said, 'They rode due south.'

'Kansas,' guessed Tom.

Walt nodded. Yeah, Kansas. Bowman would want to clear the state line by the most direct route. But, not expecting pursuit from a man he'd left for dead, and knowing that someone here would have to ride fifty miles or more before they could summon help, he wouldn't be pushing himself or his men to do it. He could only hope that these things would give him an important advantage: the element of surprise.

'Matt,' he said. 'Ellie's takin' Joey back to her hotel room. You go over to the church an' let her know you're all right.' He looked at Tom. 'You take good care of my boy here, Tom.'

'Be proud to.'

He squeezed Matt's shoulder again and said quietly, 'I'll get Sam back, son, I promise.'

And, as if to prove it, he stuffed a handful of Sam's favourite rainbow-coloured strap candy into his gunnysack before he left the store.

Bowman led his men south through the long darkness hours, with Sam – *Red* as he now thought of him – shoved face-down across his lap, crying softly. They rode in a single, strung-out line across flat, star-lit prairie, moving at a steady, unhurried gait and, as the farm fell behind them and the

165

Kansas line beckoned somewhere up ahead, he felt a savage kind of exhilaration rise up within him, for not only had he finally reclaimed his son, he'd also settled things with the farmer with whom he'd tangled earlier that evening.

He took a rare pleasure in both accomplishments, because they proved that he was still a man to be reckoned with, and for the first time in too long, he found himself actually looking forward to the future. These last few years had been a flat, thankless time. His life had been without meaning or purpose. Somewhere, somehow, he had lost his drive, his ambition, *everything*. But now it was back, all of it. He had a son now, and, like any father, he wanted to make that son proud of him.

As the night wore on, he relived the raid on Freedom Rock with a deep sense of satisfaction. The next time those townspeople talked about Arch Bowman, it would be with fear and respect and maybe just a touch of dread. He liked the sound of that. But Lord, it had been a long day and an even longer night, and he was tired. He guessed that the fist-fight had taken more out of him than he cared to admit.

He watched false dawn streak the eastern

sky with long grey streamers and knuckled at his scratchy eyes. In his lap, Red had stopped crying, but was still grizzling softly, and he growled, 'Hush up, boy. You're givin' me a headache.'

'I want my pa,' wailed the boy.

'I *am* your pa.'

'N-no you're not.'

Bowman grabbed the collar of the boy's nightshirt and pulled him up so that he could look him in the face. 'Listen to me,' he rasped. 'That other feller, he wasn't your pa, he was jus' … lookin' after you, that's all, 'til I could come back an' fetch you.'

Refusing to believe that, Sam whispered miserably, 'I want to go home.'

'Well, you can't,' Bowman said harshly. 'Leastways, not back to that place you *call* home. I'm gonna set you up someplace else, Red. Someplace real fancy. You won't want for anythin', boy. My word on it.'

'*Please* take me home,' said Sam.

His temper slipping, Bowman shoved him back face-down across his lap. 'You quit your moanin',' he snapped, 'or I'll *make* you quit.'

Ned Treber came alongside, his sabre bumping gently against his left leg. 'Kinda tough, ain't it?' he observed. 'Bein' a family man, Ah mean.'

Bowman threw him a scowl. 'I like you, Ned,' he replied. 'You're a good man to have around in a tight spot, but don't push your luck.'

Treber shrugged. 'Joshin', is all,' he said easily. In the very next moment, however, a frown creased his stern ebony face. 'You feelin' aw right, Arch? You look like hell.'

'I got a headache, is all.'

They rode on into the new day without further comment. Around them, rolling grass plains unfurled toward distant, ragged stands of elm and cottonwood. Sometime around ten o'clock, Bowman finally signalled a halt. He did indeed feel like hell, and figured the others must feel pretty much the same. After all, they hadn't eaten since the previous afternoon, and hadn't slept in damn'-near twenty-eight hours.

'Ed,' he slurred, grabbing a fistful of Sam's nightshirt and lowering the boy to the ground, 'get a fire goin'. I figure we'll rest the horses awhile.' He reached into one saddle-bag and produced the shirt, pants and boots he'd taken from the chair beside the boy's bed the night before. 'Here, get dress–'

Stiffening suddenly, he froze in the act of

168

throwing the clothes down to the wide-eyed, pale-faced boy. 'You aw right, Red?' he asked urgently. 'You hurt yourself?'

Following his gaze, Sam looked down at the front of his nightshirt, which was smeared with blood, and said nervously, 'N-no, sir.'

Realization came then, and Bowman pulled back the left side of his duster to reveal a red blotch staining his shirt. His mouth flattened out, and he muttered irritably. 'Wound's come open again, dammit.'

While Sam dragged off his nightshirt and climbed into his clothes, Bowman tore open his shirt. Somehow, he'd ruptured the thin, wrinkled, pink-purple skin that had grown over the bullet-hole: most likely it had happened during the fight, when that damn' farmer had caught him a lucky blow right over the site of the wound.

'Looks like Ah better stitch you up agin,' noted Treber, edging his mount closer.

'I'll be aw right,' Bowman said a little breathlessly.

'The hell you will. You' lost a mite a' blood awready.'

'I'll make it.'

Treber scanned the surrounding country-side with a heavy sigh. 'We tuckered, Arch,' he said at last. 'All of us. Ah say we look aroun' for someplace to hole up awhile.'

Bowman sneered at him. 'That a fact?' he asked. 'An' whereabouts you suggest we do this holin' up, Ned?'

Treber gestured away to the south-east. 'Over there.'

Bowman squinted in that direction. Sitting on the distant horizon, he could just make out the grey outline of some low frame buildings, maybe a small ranch or farm. He studied the place for a long, thoughtful moment before finally shaking his head. 'Naw. We can't spare the time. Best we push on to the state line.'

Treber sucked air in through his teeth. 'Arch,' he counselled more firmly. 'Whether you like it or not, you' goan have to rest up awhile – 'cause if you don't, you ain't goan live long enough to see that boy o' yourn become a man.'

Considering that, Bowman put his eyes back on the distant cluster of buildings. A long moment later, he said, 'Charlie, go check that place out. Quiet-like.'

Without taking his first cigarette of the day from his mouth, Breen touched spurs to his mare's flanks and said, 'On my way.'

'She ... she *will* be all right, w-won't she, Miss – uh, I mean, Ellie?'

Ellie, seated on the edge of the lumpy hotel bed, turned to study the sleeping girl's nervous-looking brother, who was hovering impotently at her shoulder. Poor Matt, she thought. He looked so frightened, and was trying so manfully to hide it, that her heart went out to him. 'Of course she will,' she replied, sounding as confident as she possibly could in order to set his mind at rest. 'The doctor said she had a mild concussion, that's all. All she needs is rest – and we'll make sure she gets it.'

He shrugged, not altogether convinced, and wandered over to the window, where he looked down into the still-deserted street below. 'I guess.'

It was early afternoon, and Walt had been gone for three hours. After he'd left the church, Ellie had wrapped Joey in a blanket and carried her up to the hotel, where she'd put her to bed and watched over her ever since. It was only when Matt had turned up at her door thirty minutes later that she discovered that Walt had gone after Sam's kidnappers. Since then, it had been an interminable, worrying time for both of them.

171

Now, she watched Matt as he peered out through the screen of thick lace and imperfect glass. He had much of his father in him, she thought; the same earnest sincerity, consideration for others and the genuine need to do what was good and right.

She stood up and went to join him. 'You must be tired out,' she offered gently. 'Why don't you try to get some rest? I'll call you the moment Joey comes round.'

He made that awkward, restless shrugging motion all over again. 'Thanks, but – I'm not tired. Couldn't sleep, anyway, for thinkin' 'bout my pa.'

'You love him very much, don't you, Matt?'

Without looking at her, he said huskily, 'Yes'm.' Then, 'I don't know what we'll do if he doesn't come back to us.'

No, she told herself. Neither do I.

Just then there came a low stirring of bedsprings, and they both turned away from the window as Joey struggled to sit up, rubbing tiredly at her eyes.

'Joey!' cried Matt.

Scared and confused, the girl looked from one of them to the other, and then her face screwed up and she started to cry. In an instant, Ellie was beside her, gathering her into strong, comforting arms and muttering, 'There … there … it's all right…'

At first the girl stiffened at her touch, but then she softened and allowed Ellie to hug her a little closer and rock her gently back and forth, all the while telling her that she was safe now, that she was going to be all right, and after another brief hesitation, Joey's arms came up and held Ellie, too, and in that moment a barrier came down and a bond of sorts was forged between them.

'There … there…' Ellie whispered into the girl's rich brown hair. But all she could think about in that moment was Walt, and what Matt had just said about him: I don't know what we'll do if he doesn't come back to us.

# EIGHT

Walt, now forking a heavily muscled sorrel horse with three white socks, moved at a steady lope through the hot, airless afternoon.

The events of the last three days had left him numb, but not so numb that he couldn't still feel sick with worry every time he thought about Sam. He tried to find comfort in what Ellie had told him earlier, that Bowman wouldn't harm the boy, and he certainly believed this to be true, but Sam wasn't to know that. He'd be scared out of his wits, wanting only his home and loved ones.

It tore him apart to think about what the boy must be going through right now, and the urge in him to push his mount to even greater speed was almost overwhelming, but somehow he forced himself to hold them both to the same mile-eating pace, knowing he must conserve the sorrel's energy, as indeed he must conserve his own.

The brassy, westering sun hammered

175

against his taut shoulders, and the cut in the back of his head started throbbing again, but he told himself that these were the least of his problems, and continued trending south. At length, the setting sun turned a deeper shade of orange and he drew rein, not really knowing where the day had gone to, but aware that he must find a place to rest up before full dark threw its velvet-and-diamond cloak across the land.

Around him, the countryside was all prairie but for a small, incongruous bosque of elm which thrust skyward about half a mile to the east. Hating the thought of giving up the chase, but still having reason enough to see the folly in blundering on into the night, he reluctantly turned them towards it.

Some time later, he built a small fire and boiled coffee, then sat with his back to a tree, sipping the bitter brew and thinking about everything that had happened to him recently. It was hard to believe that so much could change in so short a space of time. He thought about the friends he'd lost, how he'd never shoot the breeze with Pat Patterson again, or Bill Summerfield and Bernie Wilkes, and their loss was like a pain in him. Most of all, though, he thought about Sam. He couldn't *not* think about him.

He didn't sleep much that night – he hadn't for one moment imagined that he would – but he did sleep some, and he was up before the sun next morning, feeling much clearer in the head and more determined than ever to rescue his son. He wolfed down some chipped beef, eating automatically and for no other reason than that he knew the food would keep him going, then saddled up. Man and horse quit the bosque while the sky was still dark.

The sun rose and the miles unwound beneath them, and though Sam continued to dominate his thoughts, Walt was still very much aware of everything around him. He shortened rein once, when a cluster of horse-apples half-buried in flattened grass marked the spot where a mount had evacuated its bowels on the move. He was no tracker, but it was clear that the droppings were barely more than a day old.

Encouraged by the discovery, he kept going.

As the morning wore on, the broad, lifeless flats began to rise and then dip in a series of lazy undulations, and there grew more in the way of brush and timber. Then, around the middle of the morning, he spotted something white up ahead and a little to his left, caught on a low-growing shrub and flapping in the warm south-westerly wind. With a hammering heart, he quickly quartered towards it.

He had a vague idea what it was even before he drew down and threw himself out of his borrowed saddle. Leaving the horse ground-hitched, he stumbled forward, fell to his knees and tore it from the bush.

It was Sam's nightshirt.

And there was blood smeared all over it.

All at once he started shaking: he just couldn't help it. Blood ... what did it mean? What else *could* it mean? What had they done to his boy?

He staggered to his feet, feeling sick and jumpy and angry, and was just turning back to the sorrel – he didn't quite know why – when he spotted a small cluster of buildings to the far south-east.

He froze. He was looking at what folks still called the old Traynor place. Wes Traynor had ranched there for a dozen years until his early death from lung fever, at which time his distraught widow had sold every head of beef she owned and paid their hired men off. According to what they managed to piece together later, Mary Traynor had spent the next week just sitting and brooding about her man – drinking too, they said – until at length, unable to face life without him, she'd put the cold barrel of Wes's ancient Colt to her temple and pulled the trigger.

The place had lain deserted ever since.

Now Walt squinted at the distant outline, working the bloodied nightshirt slowly between his fingers. Gradually he grew less frantic and more rational. He told himself that maybe things weren't quite the way they looked. Supposing there'd been an accident, a fall, perhaps, in which Sam had been injured? If that was the case, where better to treat the boy and let him heal up than in that long-forgotten place?

He knew it was a pretty thin hope, but was equally aware that it was the only hope he had. He stared across at the dilapidated ranch for another few moments, then made up his mind to at least check it out. Rolling the nightshirt into a ball, he stuffed it into one saddle-bag, then tethered the sorrel loosely to some brush and dragged the Marlin rifle from its sheath.

He approached the place in a shambling kind of crouch-trot to avoid detection, with the rifle – long, heavy and unfamiliar in his hands – held slantwise across his chest. As the ranch came closer through a screen of tall grass, scrub and spindly trees, he saw the back of a high barn with missing planks and shingles and, just beyond it, a low bunkhouse and cookshack separated by a narrow, covered dog-trot, and a two-storey house with a rock fireplace climbing up one side wall, and a sagging porch out front, all three built around a wide, weed-cluttered yard.

The Traynor place had a lonely, forlorn look to it. Weathered corral-posts leaned drunkenly. A few empty barrels lay on their sides, and the windmill that reared up behind the bunkhouse looked just about ready to collapse, its metal blades rusted red and stuck fast.

As near as he could tell, the ranch – still a hundred yards distant – was deserted, but he knew he couldn't trust to appearances alone: he had to make sure. The first thing he must do was check out the barn. If Bowman really *had* sought shelter here, he and his men would have quartered their horses there first.

He had gone perhaps another eighty feet when a hard voice a short way to his left suddenly said, 'Hold it.'

He froze.

The man who'd gotten the drop on him stood in tree-shade about fifteen feet away. Walt saw that he was short and stocky, with a square, boyish face and peculiarly dangerous blue eyes. Recognizing him as Charlie Breen, and realizing that the man must have been watching his oh-so-cautious approach for some time, his shoulders suddenly dropped.

With recognition mutual, Breen came out into the sunglare and said easily, 'Shuck that rifle, farmer.'

Walt hesitated briefly, wondering if he could possibly shoot Breen before Breen shot him. He didn't think so. A moment longer he waited, weighing and gauging, and then he extended the Marlin to arm's length and dropped it into the tall grass, after which Breen swaggered in closer and tore the .45 from the waistband of his trousers. As he stepped back a pace, he stuffed the weapon behind his gunbelt and said around a wolfish grin, 'Thought you was dead.'

Hoping Breen might still have some charity left in him, Walt gasped desperately, 'For God's sake, I ... I've only come for my boy.'

'*Arch's* boy, you mean.'

'Please—'

Without warning, Breen lashed out with the gun in his fist, smashing him a heavy, stinging blow across the jaw. Walt grunted, described a violent half-twist and went down to one knee, breathing hard and spitting blood.

'Get up,' grated the gunman.

Playing for time, Walt said hoarsely, 'Wh-what about my boy? Is he all right?'

'He's fine,' said Breen, gesturing impatiently with his Peacemaker. 'Now do like I say, farmer. Get up, an' get movin'.'

Still Walt held his ground, willing himself to think of some way out of his predicament. If he allowed Breen to take him to Bowman, Bowman would finish him for good. And if Bowman did that, there'd be no chance at all for Sam.

He glanced up at his captor, Breen grinned back at him, a cold, harsh grin that perfectly matched the cold harshness of his very pale eyes. In his mind, he remembered what Tom Hardin had told him the day before. *Don't give the bastards any chance at all.* He knew he couldn't afford to. So, with a placating nod, he started to push back to his feet.

He got about halfway up and then

punched Breen right in the groin.

The blow had everything in it that Walt could muster, most potent of all a sudden, consuming desire to make Breen and Bowman and all the others pay for what they'd done to his family, his friends and his town. As Breen lifted to the tips of his boots and swore a high, bitter curse, he powered up to his full height, grabbed the man's gun-hand and swung him in a tight circle, then let him go. Breen's momentum sent him careening into the trunk of one of the slim cottonwoods behind which he'd so recently been hiding, and he hit hard, then bounced off, with disturbed leaves dropping around him like flat green snow.

Still angry – so angry that he was actually a little crazy with it – Walt grabbed him by one shoulder, spun him around, batted the Peacemaker out of his nerveless hand and then started to hit him, his punches a wild, brutal flurry that sent Breen staggering deeper into the timber, and all he could think, over and over again, was *Don't give the bastards any chance at all.*

He didn't plan to.

As he continued to advance, so Breen continued with his drunken, stumbling retreat, his face slack and sweaty and blood dribbling from his mouth. Then, right out of the blue, Breen blocked a punch, blocked a second, and then started fighting back. He caught Walt directly above the left eye with a wicked hook smashed him midway between chin and throat with a granite right, and in less time than it takes to tell, the odds had changed, and all at once Walt was the one backing up and defending.

Breen, consumed by fury himself now, came in like a twister. Walt managed to block two, three, maybe five punches, but he couldn't block the lot, there were too many of them. He tripped, stumbled, went down hard, and before he could regain his footing, Breen booted him in the side, kicked him again, once more.

Walt made a desperate snatch at one of his driving feet and missed. Breen kicked him again – the pain of it was indescribable – and then, still swearing hard, he tore Walt's Colt from where he'd stuffed it behind his gunbelt and rasped bloodily, 'Say so-long, farmer!'

Walt curled in on himself to present as small a target as possible, but even as he did so he heard a swift, wild rustling of grass somewhere behind them, and then a grunt of surprise that was followed by a low, meaty whack. A gunblast shattered the muggy forenoon, dirt and fallen leaves exploded not eight inches from where Walt had folded his hands over his head ... and then Charlie Breen collapsed across his legs.

He didn't move again.

Shaking hard, wondering what in hell had just happened, Walt pushed the man aside, unfolded his long frame and looked up.

His face slackened.

'Matt,' he croaked. *'Ellie!'*

They were the last people in the world he'd been expecting to see, the boy breathing hard and staring at him through scared eyes, Ellie standing beside him with a pale face and shocked features, his discarded rifle held in her tiny hands like a club, and blood shining wetly on the stock.

'What...?' he began, rising shakily. 'Where...?'

Ignoring him, still staring at the boy, Ellie stammered, 'Is he...? I mean, did I k-kill him?'

Still not thinking straight, Walt bent to take a look. The flattened, soggy patch in the crown of Breen's hat told its own story. Reaching out to take the rifle away from her, he said gently, 'Uh-huh.'

She looked a little weak. 'Oh, God.'

'He had it comin',' he pointed out. Then, as much to stop her thinking about what she'd just done as to satisfy his own curiosity, 'Where ... where did you two spring from, anyway?'

'We had to come after you, Pa,' Matt said apologetically, and threw a quick, nervous glance around them. 'Couldn't let you face these varmints on your own, neither one of us.'

Walt shook his head. Unable to phrase a complete sentence, he could only manage, 'Joey?'

'She came to yesterday afternoon,' said the boy. 'She's gonna be fine, Pa. But me, I couldn't stop frettin' 'bout you.'

'He was beside himself, Walt,' said Ellie, recovering a little. She was dressed in tough jeans and a boy's check shirt, and looked as if she'd lived all her life out on these isolated plains. 'And so was I. So we decided to leave Joey with Mr and Mrs Hardin, and ... come after you. Mr Hardin gave us the use of a wagon and we travelled practically the entire night to catch up with you.'

'Where's the wagon now?'

'We left it back there, with your horse.'

Walt shook his head some more. 'Matt, I

186

understand,' he muttered. 'He always did worry 'bout his pa, but you…?'

Abruptly, colour came back into Ellie's cheeks. 'Back in Freedom Rock, Dr Collins called me your woman,' she said, suddenly standing taller somehow. 'I liked the sound of that.'

He stared at her, understanding what she was really saying and drawing strength from the words. But almost immediately his thoughts turned back to the old Traynor place, and Sam. 'They've holed up in yonder ranch,' he said, half to himself. 'An' now, thanks to this sonofabuck, the rest of 'em know I'm comin'.'

'*We're* comin',' corrected Matt.

'Oh, no. You two've already done enough.'

'We're here, Walt,' said Ellie, determinedly. 'And we're staying.'

He looked from one to the other, knowing there was no time to argue about it. 'Even if it means more killin'?' he asked gravely.

'Even then,' she whispered.

'Then let's get to it,' he said, and pumped a bullet into the Marlin's breech.


'Wh-wh-what was that?' asked Ed Craven, rushing nervously to one busted, tar-paper window.

It was, of course, a dumb question. They all knew what it was: a gunshot. What he'd really meant was, *Who triggered it, and why?* But no one had any answer to that, yet.

As Ned Treber and Ace Hotchkiss joined him at the window, their narrowed eyes searching the empty yard, and the even emptier plains beyond, Craven started scratching at his brittle whiskers. Behind them, Bowman snapped, 'Well?'

Still weak from blood-loss, he'd been dozing against his upturned saddle in the far corner of what had once been Mary Traynor's parlour. Now it was just an empty room with dust on the floor and cobwebs straggling from the low ceiling, and it smelled very badly of damp. Sam was huddled in the opposite corner, arms clasped around his knees, his red hair awry, his tear-smeared face white and scared.

'Can't see nothin',' muttered Treber.

'No sign o' Charlie?' They'd all taken a turn at keeping watch since they'd been here: this morning had been Breen's stint.

'Nothin' a-tall, Arch. Nothin' a-tall.'

'W-w-well, that g-gunshot didn't fire itself,' said Craven.

That much being true enough, Bowman climbed awkwardly to his feet. He'd undergone some more of Treber's rough-and-ready surgery about twenty-four hours earlier, but the wound still felt sore and the repair itself somehow temporary. He shambled across the dismal room and peered through the window on the far side of the door, but as Treber had already informed him, there was nothing to see, anywhere.

'Y-you reckon it's a p-posse?' asked Craven.

Ignoring him, Bowman said, 'Ace, take a shin up that windmill out back, see what you can spot. Rest o' you fellers, look to your guns, just in case.'

With a nod, Hotchkiss turned away, grabbed up his Winchester shotgun and strode through the old wreck of a house to the back door. Cautiously, he let himself out into a small backyard where a flourishing vegetable garden had long since grown into a mess of choked-up weeds. He looked left, then right, saw no one, heard no one, and cat-footed across the yard to the windmill.

When the structure towered crookedly above him, he tucked the shotgun under one arm and started to climb the weathered wooden maintenance ladder that had been nailed to one side. Halfway up, one of the

189

rotting rungs broke underfoot with a snap like a bone-break, and he cursed but kept climbing. Five minutes later, he was sharing the narrow, gently swaying platform with the rusted, seized-up metal blades, turning his gaze slowly from one point of the compass to the next.

The prairie was quiet and empty. He wondered briefly if Charlie had busted off a cap by accident, or maybe seen and shot a snake. God knew, the damn' kid loved to use his gun. Spitting, he took another slow, thorough look around, satisfying himself that there was nothing to the north, nothing to the east, nothing to the south, nothing to the–

The minute he swung west, a tall, lean man in a collarless white shirt and dusty black pants came around the corner of the barn with a rifle in his fists, and Ace had just enough time to mutter an oath and bring his shotgun to his shoulder before the rifle gave a boom and a buck.

Down below, Walt had been alerted to rubber-faced man's position by the crack of the rotten ladder-rung, and immediately decided to abandon his quiet, cautious approach in order to whittle the Bowman bunch down still further. Not stopping to agonize over the rights and wrongs of killing, knowing that here and now it was kill or be killed, simple as that, he came around the side of the barn, snap-aimed and fired.

The Marlin's recoil smacked him hard in the shoulder, but his aim was good – that was down to pure, blind luck – and the heavy .45-.70 bullet flew true. Ace Hotchkiss jerked a tad and dropped the shotgun. Walt heard it hit the platform with a heavy clunk, saw blood spurt from a high chest-wound.

In the next moment, Ace grabbed the metal blades to steady himself, and it worked for a moment until Walt, still remembering Tom Hardin's advice, drew another bead and shot him again.

Hotchkiss reared back, yelled something weird and unintelligible, then fell forward off the platform, turning in a slow, graceful somersault before slamming head-first into the hardpan at its base.

Inside the house, Bowman snarled, 'It's him – the *farmer!*' And then, 'Get the bastard!'

Surprise and disbelief made his deep voice rise a notch.

He thrust his gun-arm through the busted

window and started emptying the gun itself at the man by the corner of the barn, his teeth clamping in fury. Treber moved to the door, opened it a crack and followed suit, and at the window on his far side, Craven added the throaty blast of his Remington to the fusillade.

Walt, meanwhile, had started moving the minute Hotchkiss fell from the windmill platform. Trouble was, he'd left it just a mite too late.

He'd taken maybe five paces toward the open barn door when something hot and hard bored into his right arm just above the elbow and shunted him sideways, against the flimsy wall. He staggered, stumbled, dropped the Marlin and kept going and, as he vanished into the barn, so the bark and snarl of lead gradually tailed off, and he thought he heard someone yell, '*G-g-got the bastard!*'

Inside the ranch house, Bowman quickly reloaded his .44, not once taking his dark glassy eyes off the barn doorway. In the corner, Sam was whimpering softly.

'*G-g-got the bastard!*' Craven yelled again.

Turning on Sam, Bowman barked, '*Quit your bawlin', damn you!*'

'You *winged* 'im, Ed,' corrected Treber,

adding meaningfully, 'So Ah guess you're the one better get on over there an' finish him off.'

'Hey, now!' began Craven, suddenly sobering.

'What you worried 'bout?' asked Treber. 'He's yourn fer the takin', man! Sonofabitch got no other weapon on him, an' likely hurtin' too much to put up a fight, anyways. He's a rat in a barrel.'

'Wh-why don't you go on over th-there, then?'

''Cause it's like you jus' said: *you* got 'im.'

'He's right, Ed,' rasped Bowman. 'Man who got him oughta finish him.'

Craven put his single, nervous eye back on the barn. When they put it like that, it didn't seem like he had a whole lot of choice about it.

He asked himself how dangerous a wounded man could be. An unarmed, wounded man, at that. He threw another uncertain, lip-chewing glance at his companions. They were both watching him expectantly, knowing he'd never really have the grit to stand up and finish the job, because he never had before.

It irritated him that they knew him so well, and he tugged furiously at his beard, hating his own lack of courage. But maybe he could still surprise them, prove them wrong. Wounded, he thought. Unarmed. Suddenly he backed away from the window and hustled to the door. 'Aw right,' he stammered. 'I d-don't guess this'll t-take long.'

As Treber stepped aside, he peered across the yard. The last of the echoes had died by now, and the ranch was cloaked in silence again. Fisting his Remington, he stepped out onto the porch, ready to drop behind a nearby, dry-as-a-bone trough at the first sign of trouble.

But there was no trouble, just the same, cloying silence, and after another moment, he started over to the barn, not daring to take his eye off the black oblong of its empty doorway.

Watching him go, Bowman hissed, 'Get around back of that barn, Ned. Make sure that idjit doesn't foul up.'

Treber's teeth showed in a quick, ivory flare. 'That damn' farmer's good as dead,' he growled.

Inside the barn, Walt hunkered low at the back of the third stall on the left and tried not to think too much about the pain in his right arm. It was hard, though. Damn' thing felt like it was on fire, and it was all he could do not to pass out.

Crouched right at the very far end of the stall, with Treber's big chestnut horse staring down at him, stamping and fidgeting at the smell of blood, he told himself he was in a hell of a fix because he'd dropped his rifle outside, and left his Colt back in the trees with Matt and Ellie.

His first thought after getting shot had been to find cover somewhere, to check how badly he'd been hit and then figure some way to keep picking off Bowman's bunch. This narrow, rotting stall had provided the cover, even if it had meant having to share it with an anxious and inquisitive horse. The wound was bad but, as near as he could tell, could've been worse, and the only way he could see to keep chipping away at his son's abductors was to creep out the back way, reclaim his Colt and come back for another crack at them.

Gradually the pain began to subside a bit, until it was just a low, persistent combination of throb and ache. When he reached the trees – *if* he reached the trees – he'd have to rig up some kind of tourniquet to stop the bleeding. He held back for a few moments more, just to gather his strength for the coming dash, then–

Suddenly, he stiffened. He'd caught the soft, hesitant shuffle of a man approaching slowly from the yard. He tried to quieten his breathing, which had grown loud with pain and nerves, and asked himself what the hell he was going to do now.

The barn doorway darkened as Ed Craven slowly came inside, pistol in hand, eye shuttling to left and right, to the doorless opening at the far end of the building and then up to the loft. Quartered horses looked back at him uneasily, associating him with all the gunfire.

'G-give it up, mister,' he grunted, addressing thin air. 'I kn-k-now you're hurtin' b-bad, an' I can fix that. B-but you try'n hide from me, I'm gonna g-get mad.'

As he spoke, he worked his way slowly down the central aisle, past the first stall, past the second … and just as he drew level with the third, a wisp of breeze-blown hay suddenly drifted down from above. His nerves already stretched tight, he leapt to the obvious conclusion, tilted the .44-.40 in his fist and sent three fast shots up into the loft.

'G-got you, you s-sonofabitch!' he yelled.

Watching him from the far end of the third stall, flinching at the nearness of the gunblasts, Walt thought, *No you haven't. Leastways, not yet. But it's only a matter of time.*

Holding his breath, he kept watching Craven's profile. The man continued staring up into the shadowy loft, his free hand constantly worrying at his tobacco-stained beard. Then, all at once, his manner seemed to change. He stiffened with a sudden, dawning realization. His head came down and around, and he looked past the chestnut horse's rump to the dark far end of the stall, right into Walt's face.

Seeing only a wounded, feverish-looking man, Craven's beard split with a grin. 'Th-there you are,' he said, and brought the Remington around.

Staring back at him, Walt did the only thing he could. He reached up, grabbed the chestnut's glistening forearm muscle between thumb and forefinger, pinched and then twisted, hard.

The horse, already jumpy, reacted instinctively. With a whinny of protest, it kicked out with its hind legs – and smashed Ed Craven right in the face.

It was a dreadful blow, and it was accompanied by a dreadful, wet, chopping sound. The owlhoot staggered backwards, his neck almost certainly broken and his shattered features suddenly obscured by a mask of blood, and then he turned, already dead on his feet, and discharged his pistol one last time into the roof before finally collapsing.

Moving quickly now, Walt came to his feet, pushed past the skittish chestnut and stepped over the still-twitching body. He threw a quick glance out into the yard, just to satisfy himself that Craven had come over here alone, then started stumble-running down to the opening at the far end of the barn, wheezing now, and drenched in sweat.

He was almost there when a soft, grass-ruffling sound just the other side of the weathered rear wall, coupled with a sudden darkening at some of the previously sun-filled gaps between the planks, made him dodge to one side and drop to a crouch. A fraction of time later, Ned Treber hurled himself into the barn with his long-barrelled .45 thrusting out ahead of him.

'Hold it, you sonofa–!'

He went three paces before the outlaw instinct in him warned him that the man he or Ed had come over here to kill was already behind him, and even as he started wheeling around Walt rose up and charged him with his good shoulder. He smashed Treber in the side and sent him reeling backwards, went after him and rammed him again. The black man yelled an oath at him, used his gun-hand to knock him away, and Walt lurched backwards, out of reach but not before he'd closed his left hand around the handle of Treber's cavalry sabre and wrenched it from its sheath.

Treber turned to face him head-on, his dark eyes hooded, his nostrils flared, his mouth a murderous, down-turned horse-shoe of absolute hatred. There was a split second when they just glared at each other – then Treber raised his .45 and pulled the trigger.

Walt thought, That's it: it's over. But the shot was hurried and smacked into one of the thin planks above and behind him, and ignoring the closeness of it, he came charging in again, the savagery and persistence of his attack paralysing Treber for one fateful moment longer.

Another brief clash of looks passed between them. Then sunlight flickered briefly along the blade of the sabre as Walt thrust it forward as quickly and forcefully as he could. Before Treber could do anything to avoid it, the weapon sliced through his butternut shirt, snagged briefly on his ribs, scraped between two of them and bored on through muscle and organ before erupting from his back.

As blood started welling around the entry-and-exit wounds, the black man's eyes widened in shock. He looked down at the sabre with something like horror, dropped his pistol and made a weak, ineffectual grab at the handle.

Walt could only watch as his mouth opened and closed and he breathed something that sounded like, 'Aahhh...' Blood accompanied the word, flecking his lips like red spit, and his skin began to turn grey.

A moment later, he fell sideways, kicked a bit and then lay still.

Walt staggered away from him, too weak and too tired to feel any revulsion at what he'd just done. All he could think of now was Sam: that four of the five men who'd taken Sam away from his family were dead, and that there was still one more with whom to deal.

He dropped lifelessly to his knees, picked up Treber's revolver left-handed and reloaded it fumblingly with rounds taken from the black man's shellbelt. Every so often he threw a glance at the ranch house across the yard, but nothing moved over there. At last he shoved back to his feet, fighting the giddiness in him and the need to puke. All that could wait, Sam came first – Sam's safety.

He stumbled back down the aisle to the front doorway. When he got there, he leaned against the frame and called in a slur. 'It's over, Bowman! The others ... they're gone!'

There was no response.

'You hear me?' Walt shouted, and suddenly he was beside himself with eagerness and fury. 'It's finished! You might as well give it up!'

Still there was no reaction, just a flat kind of echo. Then, all at once, there was a blur of movement at one of the ranch-house windows: he saw a gun-filled hand stab in his direction and a tongue of flame spit from the barrel. He heard the crash of the shot, and then his left leg was punched out from under him and he was falling.

He hit the ground hard, the impact knocking the wind out of him and jarring the .45 from his grasp. For what seemed like a lifetime there was more pain, pain just like the pain he'd already experienced, and when that subsided and he could open his tear-filled eyes and unclench his teeth again, Bowman was hobbling toward him, gun in one hand, the other snugged up tight to his left side.

Walt watched him come and had that thought again. That's it: it's over. His eyes fell to the .45 and he made a clumsy grab for it but missed. Bowman, coming closer, his shadow forging out ahead of him, quirked a cold grin at his desperate efforts.

'You're right,' he called. His voice sounded rough, bubbly, weak. 'It is over, farmer. But you lose.'

His shadow came closer over the weedy hardpan, stopping only when it covered Walt like a shroud.

'The boy's mine now,' he whispered.

Squinting up at him, Walt shook his head. 'He'll never be yours.'

With obvious difficulty, Bowman shrugged. 'Could be you're right,' he allowed. 'But one thing's for sure you won't live long enough to find out.'

As he centred his .44 on Walt's glistening forehead, the yard fell deathly quiet. As Bowman took up first pressure on the trigger, sweat fell in a trickle down the side of Walt's face. Into the silence. Bowman said, 'See you in hell, farmer.'

And that was when it happened.

There came a sound from someplace behind them, a light creaking of sagging porch-boards, and it was followed by a high, boyish yell.

'Pa!'

Recognizing Sam's voice, Bowman's finger eased up on the trigger and he thought fleetingly, and with a kind of proud wonder, Pa. He called me Pa.

It was exactly the chance Walt needed. He threw himself forward no more than six or eight inches, closed his left hand around the fallen .45, snatched it up and shot Bowman in the belly.

Bowman hunched up and instinctively pulled the trigger of his own weapon, but by then Walt had rolled out of harm's way. He came up into an awkward sitting position and shot Bowman again, this time in the throat, and Bowman went over backwards, still thinking, Pa, he called me Pa, and knowingly, deep down, that the boy had done no such thing.

He slammed to earth, aching with sorrow, and after a few minutes of gasping, finally lay still. Disturbed dust settled slowly back over his corpse.

Tired beyond words, Walt tossed the gun

away and looked around until he saw Sam standing uncertainly on the porch. Lips working then, he yelled the boy's name, held his one good arm out to him, and after the briefest hesitation, Sam came running towards him. By the time Matt and Ellie came racing into the yard, Walt was hugging Sam close and rocking the pair of them together back and forth.

'Walt!' cried Ellie, throwing herself down beside him. 'Oh God, look at you–'

'I'm all right,' he said huskily, looking into her face, with its liquid eyes and trembling lips. 'I'll be all right.'

Impulsively, she reached out and hugged him as gently as she could, and he held her with his one good arm, and the holding of her was good and right and satisfying.

They stayed like that for a long while, none of them looking at Bowman, nearby, until Matt sleeved at his wet nose and said thickly, 'I ... I'll go fetch Mr Hardin's wagon, Pa.'

Walt nodded and looked at Sam. 'You feel like goin' with him, son? You'll find some of your favourite strap candy in my gunnysack, if you do.'

The boy's face brightened and he climbed to his feet, but almost immediately, his smile was replaced by a frown. 'Will you two be all right while we're gone?' he asked seriously.

'We'll keep ourselves busy, don't you worry,' Walt replied, throwing a speculative glance at Ellie. 'I mean, we got a weddin' to plan, ain't we, girl?'

Her response was half-laugh, half-sob. 'Yes,' she replied with a blush, and reaching out to grasp his good hand, she added, 'Yes, Walt. We most certainly have.'

The publishers hope that this book has given you enjoyable reading. Large Print Books are especially designed to be as easy to see and hold as possible. If you wish a complete list of our books please ask at your local library or write directly to:

**Dales Large Print Books**
Magna House, Long Preston,
Skipton, North Yorkshire.
BD23 4ND